HOW BIG IS THE
MOON?

HOW BIG IS THE MOON?

WHOLE MATHS IN ACTION

OXFORD
UNIVERSITY PRESS

Melbourne

Dave Baker Cheryl Semple Tony Stead

OXFORD UNIVERSITY PRESS AUSTRALIA

Oxford New York Toronto
Delhi Bombay Calcutta Madras Karachi
Kuala Lumpur Singapore Hong Kong Tokyo
Nairobi Dar es Salaam Cape Town
Melbourne Auckland
and associated companies in
Berlin Ibadan

OXFORD is a trade mark of Oxford University Press

First published 1990
Reprinted 1992

National Library of Australia
Cataloguing-in-Publication data:

Baker, Dave.
How big is the moon?: whole maths in action.

Bibliography.
ISBN 0 19 553135 3.

[I]. Mathematics — Study and teaching (Primary).
I. Semple, Cheryl. II. Stead, Tony. III. Title.

372.7044

Designed by David Rosemeyer
Typeset by Solo Typesetting, South Melbourne
Printed by Impact Printing Victoria Pty Ltd
Published by Oxford University Press,
253 Normanby Road, South Melbourne, Australia

Contents

Introduction

During 1987 we became very dissatisfied with our maths program, largely as a result of the comparisons we made between it and our language program.

We felt that our language program was very effective in providing stimulating, interesting and challenging experiences for our students. These experiences were enabling children to develop the skills of proficient language users. The children were responding very well to the program and we felt good about it too!

When it came to maths it was a different story. We were less confident with maths and it showed. The children were not stimulated, interested or challenged and we felt uncomfortable about the approach we were using in our teaching and the content we were offering.

We believed that our language program was successful because it was based on sound learning principles, so we decided to transfer these principles to our maths program. This change in approach had far-reaching implications for the content of our maths program and required us to rethink what we believed was important about teaching and learning maths.

We were fortunate in having Dave Baker, on exchange from Brighton Polytechnic in the United Kingdom, work with us during the year. He supported and extended our thinking about maths in schools.

The program we have outlined was developed over a period of eighteen months. It was continually revised, adapted and rewritten. As we strove to develop a program that gave the children both challenging and meaningful experiences in maths, all of us became increasingly excited about what we were doing.

We now believe that we have the basis of a program that provides children with mathematical understandings in a challenging, interesting and purposeful manner.

Cheryl Semple
Tony Stead

Chapter One
What is whole maths?

Introduction

Early in the year, before we had introduced our whole maths program, our students saw maths as sums and purposeless measurement activities. This narrow view of maths as unconnected facts to do with numbers or ways of doing pencil and paper calculations, lacked any contextual reference to their daily lives.

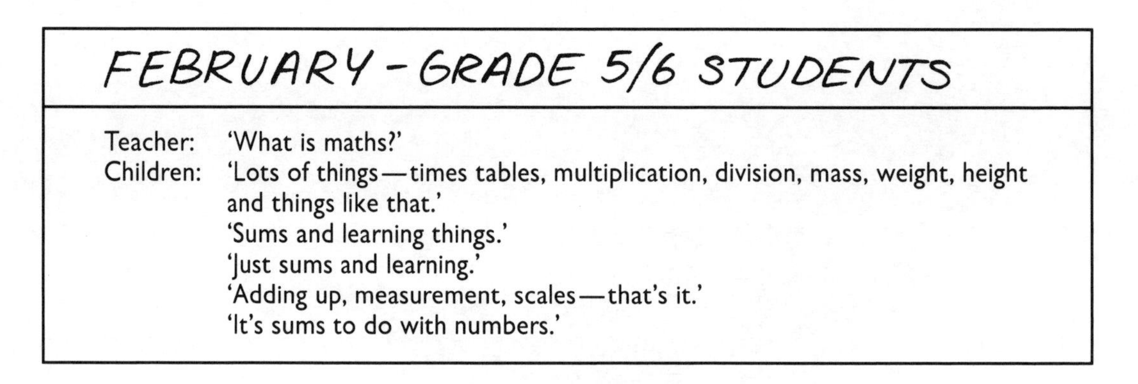

FEBRUARY - GRADE 5/6 STUDENTS

Teacher: 'What is maths?'
Children: 'Lots of things—times tables, multiplication, division, mass, weight, height and things like that.'
'Sums and learning things.'
'Just sums and learning.'
'Adding up, measurement, scales—that's it.'
'It's sums to do with numbers.'

By August, these same students had developed an understanding of maths as a relevant and purposeful life skill. Maths had become an active process in which the students were involved in the exploration of their own ideas. These students were now:

- becoming familiar with, and using, maths facts, skills and concepts;
- using processes, such as estimating, hypothesising, generalising and justifying;
- developing good work habits, such as perseverance and concentration;
- understanding the broader functions of maths outside the classroom.

They were challenged, excited and personally involved in the maths program.

AUGUST - GRADE 5/6 STUDENTS

Teacher: 'What is maths?'
Children: 'The time, volume, area—about learning and finding out things—working out solutions—you use maths everywhere you go—when you pull a chair out from a table you need to know how far to pull it out so you can fit in—that's maths.'
'Maths is using things. Maths is shopping and working out how much things are and if you have enough to pay for them—it's nearly everything—you use it at school, at home, everywhere.'
'Maths is time, it's if you go to the shop, knowing how much change to get so that you don't get ripped off. Maths is being able to read the time, it's the seasons, the days, the months—it's knowing when it's your birthday. It helps you through your life. Maths is how long it takes the sun to go around the earth, it's volume, how to use a calculator, it's lots of things.'
'Maths is like that squares game we played . . . I played it a few times . . . then I thought there must be a way to win—so I drew a few pictures and found out a way—now I'm the grade champion.'

How did this shift come about?

Rationale

Changes in the children's attitudes towards mathematics were a direct result of the changes we made to our maths program. These were based on our clear understanding of what children should know about maths and how they learn maths.

Content

The content of our maths program was determined by our view of maths as more than the body of knowledge it is seen to be in the traditional classroom. Maths certainly includes facts, skills and concepts in number, measure, spatial relations and visual representation. But we believe it also includes using mathematical processes to solve practical and abstract problems, and it encourages the development of personal qualities such as perseverance and cooperation. We believe that maths also provides children with tools to think and to communicate with.

Our objectives thus focused on:

- the facts, skills and concepts in mathematical content;
- the processes which assist problem-solving, communicating and exploring;
- personal qualities and attitudes.

Facts, skills and concepts

FACTS are often unconnected pieces of information; when inter-related, they can become more useful, e.g. 'the sun rises in the east' as opposed to '9 × 6 = 54'.

SKILLS describe the ability to carry out well established procedures, e.g. the accurate completion of a multiplication algorithm.

CONCEPTS are generalised ideas underlying mathematics, e.g. the nature of subtraction.

Example—Addition

Fact:	6 + 3 = 9
Skill:	the accurate completion of an addition algorithm
Concept:	to add one thing to another

The processes

These include: identifying, recognising, classifying, representing, estimating, predicting, generalising, specialising, hypothesising, justifying, explaining, describing and communicating.

Personal qualities

These include: independence, perseverance, concentration, co-operation, confidence, a sense of self-esteem.

The objectives fit together like this:

FACTS SKILLS CONCEPTS	PROCESSES	PERSONAL QUALITIES
• numbers • measurement • spatial relations • visual representation	• classifying • recording • representing • explaining • describing	• work habits • relationships • cooperation with others • attitudes

Conditions for learning

1 Children learn about maths best when the maths they meet is embedded in purposeful activities; that is, when the children are *immersed* in real purposes for using and exploring maths. When adults highlight maths in the environment, children become

aware that they themselves are *immersed* in a maths environment. For example, after a silent reading session the teacher may ask children what type of material they were reading and note this on the chalkboard—recording what fraction of the grade were reading magazines, novels, newspapers or stories.

2 Children learn about problem-solving strategies such as classifying, representing and explaining when they see them *demonstrated* (by adults or other children). The wider the variety of demonstrations that children see, the more likely it is that they will see one that makes sense to them. Cooperative learning enhances children's opportunities to be both learners about, and demonstrators of strategies. Children also learn about the personal qualities employed by the demonstrator, such as perseverance and concentration.

3 Children learn when the significant adults around them *expect* them to learn. Children, especially girls, learn that they can be successful in maths when teachers *expect* that all children will succeed in exploring and solving problems. This expectation is only met, in a positive manner, when children are self-motivated rather than motivated by discipline, obedience or dependence.

4 Children need to be given the *responsibility* of choosing what and how they'll explore, who they'll work with and how they'll present their findings, in order that their learning is meaningful and purposeful to them. Children learn best when they come to terms with maths concepts in ways that make sense to them. Children will only become effective decision-makers when they are given the opportunity to make decisions about a whole range of issues.

5 Children learn to employ efficient and effective problem-solving strategies when they are encouraged, initially, to use strategies that make sense to them, while at the same time observing more efficient and more effective strategies. In this way children are *approximating* effective and efficient strategies. In acknowledging *approximation* as a relevant condition for maths learning, we are focused on the problem-solving process rather than the product.

6 Children learn best when they receive *feedback* about their explorations. *Feedback:*

- acknowledges their endeavours and tells them that what they are thinking, saying and writing makes sense; and
- extends their understandings.

7 Children learn best when they are part of a secure *environment* which encourages sharing and cooperation between its members and values each and every contribution made.*

---

*These conditions for learning are based on the work of Brian Cambourne.

Approach

Our new approach to maths draws on the best features of our language teaching and encompasses the following ideas:

- that maths has to be explored in meaningful contexts;
- that maths is more than just a body of knowledge and that it involves children in problem-solving processes and developing good work habits;
- that children need a range of skills to handle their everyday lives and that being confident about maths means children are more independent and self-sufficient;
- that children benefit from the experience of finding themselves being mathematicians when they are looking for patterns, forming generalisations and then justifying their results;
- that children need to explore maths for its own sake;
- that children need to develop a positive attitude to maths in order to effectively acquire maths skills and understandings.

Accordingly, we found it necessary to tip the model of our traditional approach on its head (as many teachers have done with their language models).

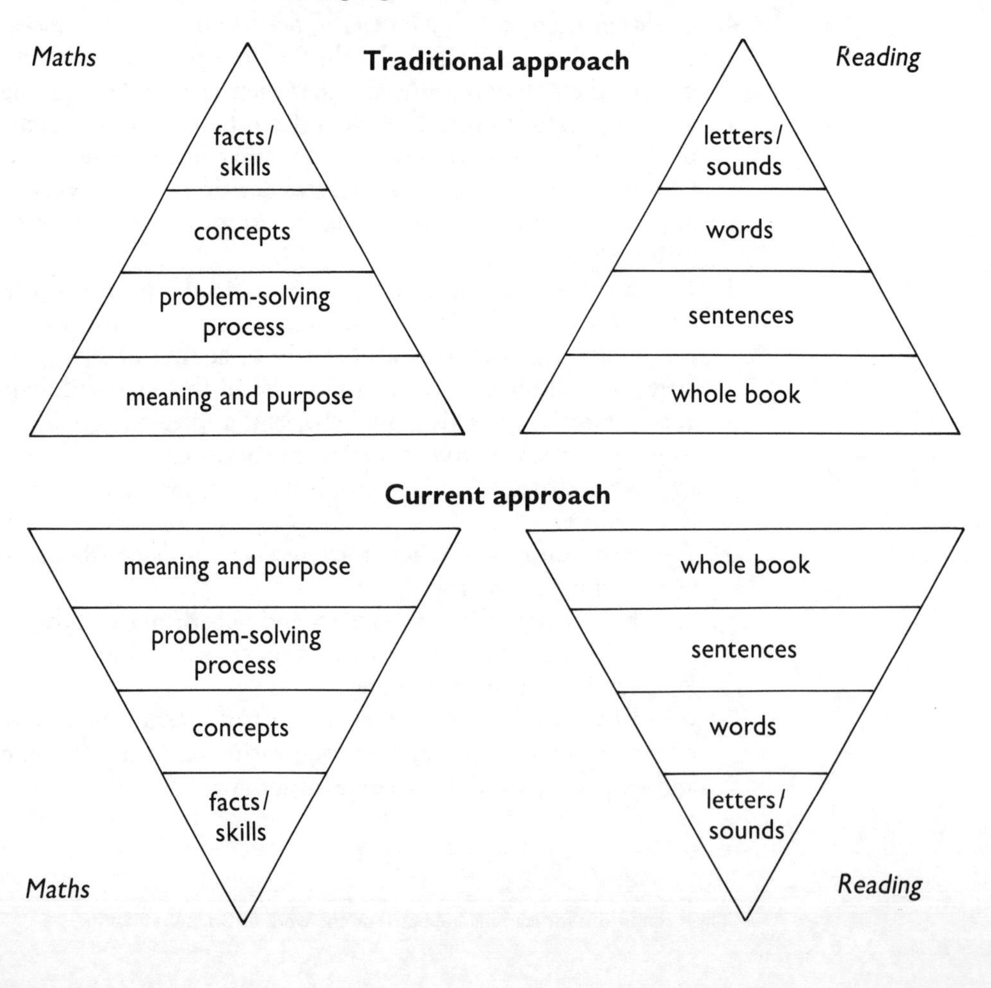

	TRADITIONAL APPROACH	CURRENT APPROACH
Demonstration	A skill is demonstrated and children are given opportunities to practise it in ways determined by the teacher.	A skill is demonstrated and children are given the freedom to use it in ways that make sense to them.
Immersion	Problem-solving often has no real purpose for children.	Children are immersed in real purposes for using and exploring maths.
Expectation	All children are not expected to succeed in maths strategies demonstrated.	Children are expected to be successful in solving their own problems in their own ways.
Responsibility	Teachers take responsibility for deciding what will be included in the content and how it will be approached.	Children take joint responsibility for the content of the subject and how it will be approached.
Approximation	Children are required to employ the strategy demonstrated.	Children take responsibility for the problem-solving strategies they use, while continually moving towards more efficient and effective strategies.
Feedback	Children receive feedback about the products of their work from the teacher.	Children receive feedback about the process and product of their work from teacher and peers.
Engagement	Children are engaged in practising how to use facts, skills and concepts.	Children are engaged in problem-solving which requires making choices about which strategies to use.
Purpose	Children are often not aware of why they are learning a specific skill.	The purpose for learning specific skills is always apparent because children start with a problem to solve.
Meaning	Problem-solving activities often have no meaning for children.	Children decide what they will explore; thus all problems have meaning for them.
Focus	Facts. Skills. Concepts.	Meaningful context.

Traditionally, in both language and maths, we have moved from the meaningless part to the meaningful whole, and children who couldn't make sense of the abstract nature of the parts fell by the wayside. There was nothing in the new learning that they could link into their existing understanding. In the part to whole approach, children who have difficulty with skills or concepts are 'stuck' with meaningless experiences. For instance, in maths, traditionally, we have taught children the basic number facts and operations, exposed them to a variety of number concepts and then presented them with problems to solve. In many cases the problems we gave them to solve were of the meaningless variety—'If apples cost 23 cents each and you bought six, how much would it cost you altogether?' If we looked carefully at how we divided our time between these issues, we would probably find that we devoted 60–70 per cent to the basic operations, 10–20 per cent to applied number and 10 per cent to problem-solving.

We have found that we can help children learn about maths best if we reverse this approach. We begin by allowing children to explore real-life problems or issues that are meaningful to them and within the context of this exploration we help them to come to terms with the relevant facts, skills, concepts and processes. In approaching maths in this way, the purpose for knowing about specific facts and skills is always evident to the child.

As the children have chosen what, how and with whom they will explore their maths topics, they are also in a position to develop the personal qualities of persevering, cooperation, and independence and to strive to develop effective and efficient processes for problem-solving. Chapter 2 gives a step-by-step description of how the model works.

A comparison of the traditional and current approaches will highlight the differences between them and demonstrate our reasons for adopting the current model. When classroom practice is based upon the principles outlined in the Current Approach, a very effective learning environment is established.

The **traditional model** is found in classrooms where children are passive learners and teachers take responsibility for all decisions relating to curriculum and methodology. The **current model** is found in classrooms where teachers have established a learning environment which encourages and expects children to take responsibility for their own learning and share in curriculum decisions. The importance of establishing a positive learning environment cannot be over estimated and must be the focus of a teacher's energies in the first weeks in a new classroom.

Chapter Two

Planning and implementation

Introduction

An effective way of producing a balanced program which stems from children's interests and develops the necessary facts, skills, and concepts, processes, and personal qualities is to operate a maths program on a five week unit basis. Children work best when they alternate between:

- teacher directed activities which model effective strategies for problem-solving and investigations; and
- child directed activities which encourage them to employ the strategies modelled.

The five week unit program was designed to cater for the individual needs of our particular children and it must be stressed that this example is only a guide. Teachers of lower grades may find that their children require more than one week for adequate modelling of effective strategies during the whole grade exploration and that three weeks is far too long for individual and small group exploration. Teachers need to assess the needs of their own children and design a unit that effectively caters for these needs.

The following diagram gives an overview of the five week unit program and is followed by a detailed account of each part of the unit under the following headings:

- aims
- getting started
- example of a unit
- activities and ideas

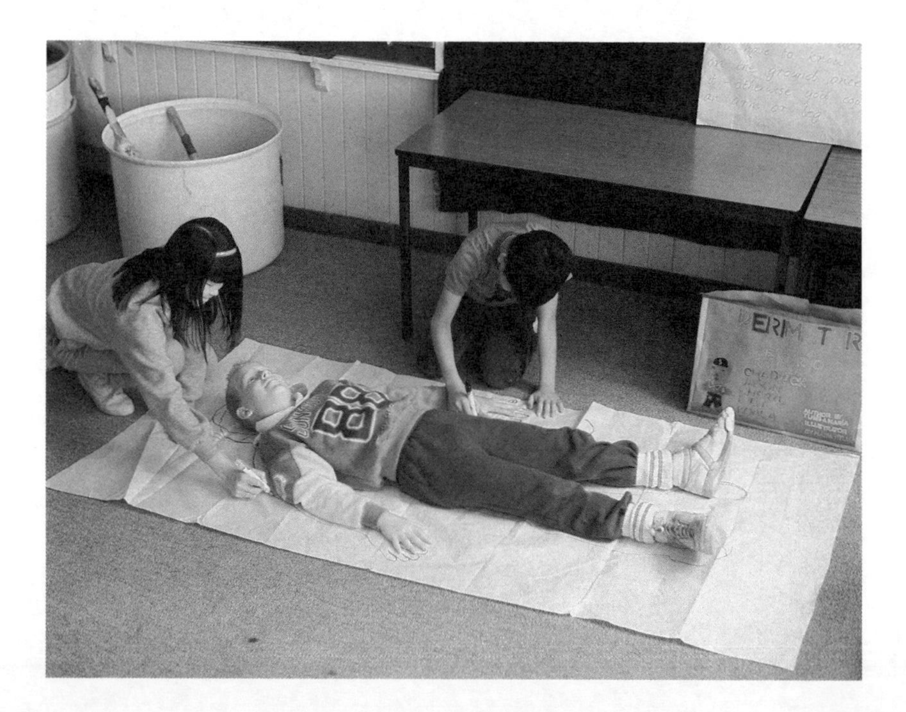

OVERVIEW OF A FIVE WEEK UNIT PROGRAM		
PART 1 *(one week)*	**Whole grade exploration** • teacher selected • based on children's needs	Teacher demonstrates: – collecting resources – gathering and recording information – presenting information – specific skills – representing and interpreting data – processing
PART 2 *(three weeks)*	**Individual/small group explorations** • child selected • based on children's interests	Children: – develop and extend their understandings – take responsibility for their own learning – develop their ability to work cooperatively
PART 3 *(one week)*	**Investigations, games and puzzles** • teacher and child selected • based on children's interests and needs	Children: – develop their use and understanding of maths processes and investigational strategies – develop work habits of reflection and perseverance – develop their awareness of the abstract nature of maths

Part 1 (one week)—Whole grade exploration

The topic for study in this section is selected by the teacher and based on the needs of the children.

Aims

- To help children develop as independent learners and thinkers by:
  - modelling methods of gathering information and resources.
  - encouraging children to gather their own resources.
  - encouraging children to make decisions.
  - demonstrating different methods of presenting and interpreting information.
- To develop the children's sense of themselves as a community of learners in which they see each other as valuable resources.
- To develop specific mathematical facts, skills and concepts, processes and personal qualities at the whole-grade level.

Getting started

- Select a topic that you feel children need to focus on—you will need to consider the extent to which your children are already confident about the skills and concepts included in your curriculum.
- Tell the children why you have selected the topic—ask their opinion about its importance.
- Plan a way of beginning the topic that takes account of the children's knowledge and interests—posing questions is a good way to start.
- Encourage children to explore the problems in their own ways—initially they may find this difficult, especially if they have always relied on the teacher to provide the appropriate strategy.
- Allow children to work in groups of their own choice—when children select their own working groups they initially choose to work with friends, but as they become more confident they begin to group themselves according to interests; e.g. late in the year we found that a grade 6 boy and a grade 5 girl chose to work together because they were both interested in planning an orienteering course.
- Discuss the types of resources that would be useful in solving these problems—ensure that they are available.

Example of a unit—Time

We chose to explore the concept of time because we felt that there were many children who were experiencing difficulties in this area. These difficulties ranged from telling the time to more complex issues such as planetary relations, the 24 hour clock, daylight savings and world time. We believed that having a sound understanding of these issues was imperative for the children.

DAY 1 - INTRODUCTION OF TOPIC

We chose to introduce the topic by posing 3 questions for the children to solve individually or in small groups. These questions were based on issues which were of particular interest to the children at this time.

1 Dave is going home to England via Perth. He wants his friends to meet him at the airport. His plane leaves Melbourne at 2.00 pm on Monday 19 December. What time should his friends meet him at the airport?
2 Maria's grandmother lives in Italy. Maria wants to ring her, but wants to make sure that she rings during the day. What time should Maria ring her grandmother?
3 Cheryl wants to ring her friend Marie in Norway. Marie is always home at 5.00 pm. What time should Cheryl ring Marie?

We gave the children 10 minutes to explore the problems, telling them that we would then gather together to discuss their findings. Some children went straight to atlases, others to dictionaries and some began to flick through encyclopaedias . . . a few children had no idea where to start and just wrote the first thing that popped into their head . . . others had relations in Italy and knew that there was a substantial time difference but didn't know what it was.

On calling the children back together one group explained that they'd found out about time zones in the encyclopaedia . . . we talked briefly about how this had helped them to find a solution. We used the telephone book (demonstrating it's potential as a resource) to question their solution.

As we discussed the children's answers to the problems it became evident that some of them had a great deal of knowledge about world time but that there were gaps in their knowledge. For instance, some children did not know whether noon was am or pm and what these symbols meant. One group attempting to solve problem one worked out that it would take three and a half hours to fly to Perth. They calculated the distance from Perth to Melbourne (using the atlas), asked the speed of jets and then, using the calculator, worked out the time for the trip.

Considerations

- Ensure that appropriate resources are always available.
- Support and direct children's explorations by:
  - i) providing frequent sharing times that allow children to explain how they are solving their problems—thus giving ideas to the rest of the grade;
  - ii) demonstrating the use of resources and ways of problem-solving.
- In exploring set problems children and teachers become aware of the extent of the children's knowledge in this area.
- Accept all problem-solving strategies used by children and discuss which are the simplest and most effective to use.
- Help children identify issues they would like to explore further.

DAY 2

Children brainstormed (in groups) what they knew about time and this was collated at the class level. Their knowledge was reasonably diverse. Children then formed groups to discuss what they would like to explore over the next two days. Names were put against issues. The children were asked to come the next day with resources and ideas ready to begin a two day exploration.

Considerations

- Acknowledge what the children know about an issue.
- Allow children to learn from each other by sharing and documenting ideas.
- Help children select an area to explore by providing an initial experience that will focus their thinking.

DAY 3

Children brought in lots of reference material to solve their problems and were eager to get going—they amazed us with their involvement in and positive attitude towards exploration. Tim, David and Carl's original problem was the time difference between countries. From this they became interested in the distance between planets, why some planets were hotter than others yet further from the sun, why we have a leap year etc. They were so engrossed in what they were doing that they wanted to explore it further during individual small group explorations. Kieu, Alex and Dimitra's original problem of the time difference between countries led them to finding out how long it would take to travel by plane to certain places in Australia . . . they had decided to write to Qantas for information.

Considerations

- Encourage children to take some responsibility for finding their own resources.
- Hold individual and small group conferences for those who need them.
- Conferencing is very important at this time in order to show the children that you are interested in their ideas and to support them in finding and interpreting information.
- Provide sharing times so that children maintain their interest and are challenged and supported by the ideas of others.
- Children's explorations will cover a diverse range of issues at a diverse range of complexity—you will often be left behind!

DAY 4

We held a clinic for telling the time from a clock face—Maria, Rosalind, Betty, Tung and Michael were all keen to learn how to tell the time. The three girls get confused by the two hands; they don't understand that the 12 hours and the 60 minutes in each hour are represented on the same circle by two different hands.

Outside the clinic Marisa created a problem and challenged David to solve it. David couldn't solve it and Marisa gleefully announced that she was going to see if Tim could solve it . . . the children were still working with enthusiasm and commitment.

Considerations

- Provide clinics on issues in which children are experiencing difficulty.
- Encourage children to challenge each other by creating problems as well as solving them.

DAY 5

All the children had solved their problems to varying degrees and had no trouble in explaining how they had accomplished this. Problem one led to a discussion on the speed of light and sound—many children found this a difficult concept to understand. Most children had information to add to the class chart on 'Everything we know about time'.

It was obvious by the amount of lively chatter that they had been very interested in, and challenged by, the problems they had worked with. Many children have explored quite complex concepts and were keen to continue working on these over the next three weeks. We made a list of topics that children had already chosen for the second part. I told the other children to think about the projects over the weekend and to come in on Monday morning with a definite idea of what they wanted to work on. I gave one group the opportunity to collate all the information we had collected on time and then to publish it . . . the children involved were receptive to this and looked forward to taking on the task.

Considerations

- Solving one set of problems leads to questions about related issues.
- Children need time to share and discuss their findings with others.
- Many children will choose to continue working on the ideas presented and explored in Part one.

Activities

A list of topics has been provided below to support you and your class in whole grade explorations in part 1 of the program. These are intended to be only a guide and a support when you first start the program or when you are short of ideas of your own. As you proceed with the program you will find many topics based on the children's immediate needs and interests. It is important to remember that the children must see the real purposes of these activities—that means topics cannot be imposed on them without their views being considered.

Suggested topics for whole grade explorations

1. How do things move? (e.g. cars, bikes, swings, parachutes, paper planes, boats, animals, people)
2. Why are computer and typewriter keyboards designed as they are?
3. Time zones across the world
4. Planning a sausage sizzle
5. Raising money to purchase something the classroom needs
6. Conducting a mini-Olympics in the classroom
7. Nationalities in our classroom
8. Similarities and differences between people in our class
9. These are a few of my favorite things
10. What's your favorite number and why?
11. What makes a rainbow?
12. The biggest things in the classroom
13. Ghosts, goblins and witches
14. My family tree
15. How many people do we all know?
16. Fire and heat
17. All about magnets
18. Countries around the world
19. Our solar system
20. How many grains in a handful of sand?

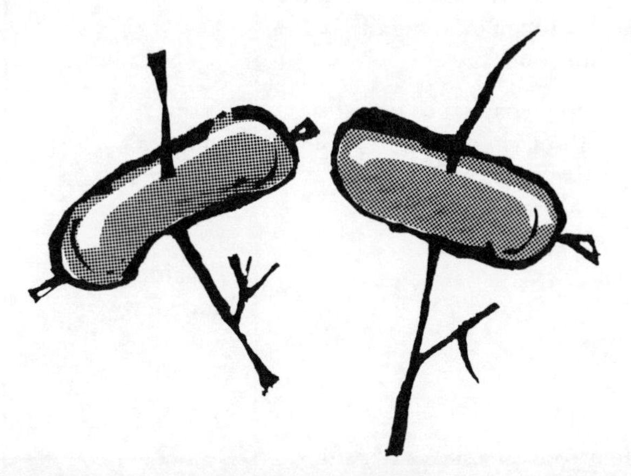

'Fermi' problems also provide a good source of ideas for whole grade explorations.

Eight topics have been developed in detail showing the steps each class will go through. The processes the children meet have been identified and the facts, skills and concepts listed. A blank planning sheet in the same format has been included for you to copy and use to record your own topics. This serves as a record of the activities carried out as well as the facts, skills and concepts explored by the children. It then forms part of your work program.

1 — Planning an excursion

ACTIVITIES/IDEAS	PROCESSES	FACTS/SKILLS/CONCEPTS
• Make a list of all the places children would like to go and why.	Identifying Classifying Describing	
• Ask children to individually vote on their personal preference, then count the votes and list the four most popular choices.	Deciding	Counting Using data
• The class brainstorms the information they will need to use for making a final choice, e.g. costing, time, reasons for going, lunch arrangements etc. These are listed on a large sheet of paper.	Identifying Estimating Reporting	Value, time, distance Estimations of money, time, distance
• Children work in groups according to their preferences to find out as much information as possible. During this time, it is essential for the teacher to move around each group to ensure that all the children are clear about the task set. Children will need a rough estimate of the cost to hire a bus.	Estimating Collecting data Recording data	Working with money Recording whole numbers and decimals Four operations on whole numbers up to three digits Four operations on decimals Checking whether results are sensible Using a calculator
• Each group prepares a chart listing all the information gathered about their particular excursion and presents this to the whole grade.	Sorting Recording Presenting Sharing Discussing Explaining Processing	Ways of representing information Use of tables Addition up to five digits Division with whole numbers Estimating time Calculations on time—working with hours and minutes Timetables
• Children vote on which excursion they would like to attend after seeing each group's chart.	Deciding	Using and interpreting data
• Once a decision has been reached, each group is responsible for a particular part of the organisation of the excursion, e.g. booking the bus, preparation of permission notes, organisation of finances, planning of follow-up work after the excursion refreshments, the day's timetable.	Estimating Preparing Planning	Operations on time and money including whole numbers and decimals Designing schedule letters, activities

2—Investigating water (floating and sinking)

ACTIVITIES/IDEAS	PROCESSES	FACTS/SKILLS/CONCEPTS
• Read *Who sank the boat* by Pamela Allen (see References). Discuss issues arising from the book, e.g. floating and sinking.	Questioning Estimating	Estimation of size Concepts of weight Early ideas of density and volume
• In small groups children record what they know about floating and sinking. Each child in the group is given a particular role to ensure group cooperation, e.g. scribe, reporter, leader, helper. Discuss each of these roles with the children.	Identifying Classifying Collecting data Recording data	Volume Weight of material Density
• Groups present findings to whole grade. These are recorded by the teacher onto a large sheet of paper.	Interpreting data Presenting findings	Calculations on data Average, totals
• Discuss the experiments with water that the children would like to explore, e.g. Will wood always float? Does the weight of an object determine whether it will sink or float? What is the heaviest object that you can make float? Does steel always sink?	Classifying materials Estimating Predicting Relating	Size and weight and their relationship
• In groups children decide which experiments they are interested in exploring.	Deciding	
• Discuss with the whole class effective ways to record experiments, e.g. hypothesis, materials needed, method, finding.	Hypothesising Recording Concluding	Methods of measuring length, volume, weight
• Set up large water containers and materials needed for experiments and allow groups to begin.		Measuring length, volume and weight Calculating from measurements Using instruments
• As each group makes a discovery, the scribe records these findings onto the large sheet of paper containing original knowledge.	Recording Justifying	
• When experiments are completed each group reports its findings to the class.	Generalising findings Reporting Presenting Explaining Convincing	Nature of floating Nature of density

3—Making furniture for the classroom

ACTIVITIES/IDEAS	PROCESSES	FACTS/SKILLS/CONCEPTS
• Brainstorm with the children what extra furniture they would like to make for the classroom, e.g. chairs, tables, cubby house, bookshelves etc.	Identifying Classifying Estimating	Length, height
• Children are grouped according to preferences and each group makes a list of factors which will need to be considered, e.g. strength, shape, comfort, looks, stability, materials needed, style, size, role of each group member etc.	Identifying factors Listing factors Relating factors Designing Deciding on qualities Relating shapes	Simple measurement of qualities like strength (stronger/weaker) or comfort Spatial relations 2D and 3D shapes
• Each group decides on the data they need to collect. They measure the sizes they need, record the information, and calculate what they need.	Collect data Measuring Recording data Processing data	Using instruments, measurements of length, weight, angles Recording measurements as whole numbers or decimals Calculating averages Using four operations
• Each group is then asked to produce a plan and presents this to the class for approval. Encourage children to question each group on exactly how they are going to go about producing the piece of furniture decided upon.	Planning Presenting Questioning and challenging	Using measurements Using diagrams and plans Scale drawings
• Once approval is given, each group commences gathering the materials and making the piece of furniture. During this time the teacher will need to assist groups in demonstrating different techniques of constructing particular items.	Making Constructing	Using instruments and measurements Using lengths and angles
• At regular intervals, it is advantageous to get each group to share particular techniques they found useful so that other groups can use these in their own constructions.	Sharing	Measuring and constructing techniques
• Once each group has made its piece of furniture these are all shared and the class decides where best to place each item in the classroom. In sharing, encourage each group to talk about the different processes they went through.	Sharing Presenting Deciding Identifying processes	Estimation of size, shape, space needed Spatial relations

4—Finding out about our class

ACTIVITIES/IDEAS	PROCESSES	FACTS/SKILLS/CONCEPTS
• Brainstorm all the things about the class the children would be interested in exploring, e.g. How many fingers in this class? If we put our bodies end to end, how long would we be? If we put our feet together would we cover the length of the classroom? How much would we weigh altogether? Children choose what they want to explore.	Classifying Identifying Estimating Conjecturing Predicting	Counting Concepts of length and weight Numbers Decimals
• In small groups of their own choosing, children discuss ways of finding out the information needed. Encourage children to come up with as many ways as possible.	Ways of collecting data Recording Creating	Methods of measuring and counting
• Each group shares its various methods of exploration with the class. These should be recorded by the teacher on paper or chalkboard.	Sharing	Methods of measuring and counting
• Each group decides which method of exploration they think will best suit their investigation, and the resources they will require.	Deciding Planning Choosing resources	
• Groups then begin the investigations with the teacher rotating around each group to give assistance. At this stage it will be necessary for groups to work cooperatively with each other so that data about each individual can be collected by each group. It may be that each group in turn is allocated a period of time to collect the necessary data from individuals in other groups. Children should be given the responsibility for organising this.	Collect data Recording data Planning and organising Designing data sheets	Recording counts or measurements Using numbers or decimals Working with different units of measurement Using a ruler Using a calculator
• Once all the data has been collected, it is processed. The children discuss various means of presenting their findings. These are listed by the teacher on the chalkboard or paper	Analysing data Presenting data	Calculating from data Find most/least averages, totals Using four operations Visual representation
• Groups then decide on their method of presentation. They interpret their results and in turn share their findings with the rest of the class.	Presenting data Interpreting results Sharing	Visual representation

ACTIVITIES/IDEAS	PROCESSES	FACTS/SKILLS/CONCEPTS
• Encourage children to question each group about the processes they went through in conducting their research. • Each group's findings are displayed under a heading, **Amazing things about our class.**	Challenging Explaining Justifying Communicating	

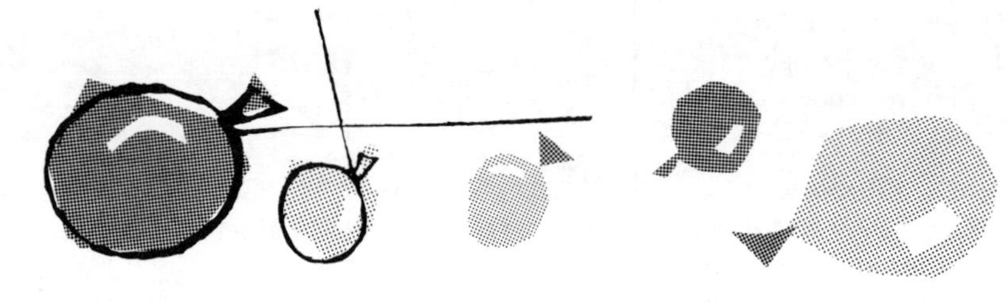

5—Planning a special event

ACTIVITIES/IDEAS	PROCESSES	FACTS/SKILLS/CONCEPTS
• Whole grade discussion brainstorming all the points which will need to be considered, e.g. costing, decorations, food preparation, activities/games, cleaning, invitations. These are recorded by the teacher on the chalk-board or a large sheet of paper. Children choose which of these they want to work on.	Identifying Sorting Classifying Deciding Estimating amounts and costs	Time Shape Money Total amounts Four operations
• Children choose their own groups. Each group lists all the factors which need to be considered for their particular area, e.g. materials needed, amount of money required, organisational details.	Classifying Sorting Listing factors Discussing	Thinking about money and time
• Once all factors have been listed, the teacher discusses with the children the concept of a time-line.	Ordering by time Recording	Time intervals Time-lines Visual representations
• Each group then draws up a time-line and allocates a specific task to each member.	Organising Planning	

ACTIVITIES/IDEAS	PROCESSES	FACTS/SKILLS/CONCEPTS
• Children then come together to discuss their roles—exactly how they are going to achieve the tasks, and how long it will take.	Organising Planning Cooperating	Time and time intervals
• Children commence organising their particular roles. Encourage children to assist each other during this process and offer advice if needed.	Sharing Supporting Collecting data Recording data	Using measurements or counting Whole numbers or decimals Money Time Shapes Making decorations Amounts of food
• It is advisable to bring the grade together at regular intervals to discuss how everything is going and to find effective ways of solving problems which may occur. Prior to these discussions, each group will need to meet to talk about issues arising and to appoint a speaker.	Identifying problems Solving problems	Using measurements or counting Whole numbers or decimals Money Time Shapes Making decorations Amount of food Using a calculator
• Just prior to the event and when everything is organised, arrange a class discussion to talk about the different processes individual children and groups went through, and ways an event could be better organised next time.	Sharing Discussing Justifying	Awareness of the ways time, space, money and size could affect the situation

6—Bubbles

ACTIVITIES/IDEAS	PROCESSES	FACTS/SKILLS/CONCEPTS
• On a large sheet of paper the teacher records **Everything we know about bubbles.**	Identifying Classifying	Shape Size Length Area
• Children brainstorm existing knowledge and this is recorded onto the sheet of paper.	Recording	

ACTIVITIES/IDEAS	PROCESSES	FACTS/SKILLS/CONCEPTS
• Demonstrate to children various ways bubbles can be formed, e.g.: a Cut a piece of string 30 cm in length. Cut a straw in half. Thread the string through the two pieces of straw. Tie the string in a knot to form a frame. 	Designing	Shapes Measurement Using a ruler Fractions
b Cut a piece of fishing line 60 cm in length. Tie the ends in a knot to form a circular shape. 		
c Bend a piece of florist wire to form a bubble-making machine. 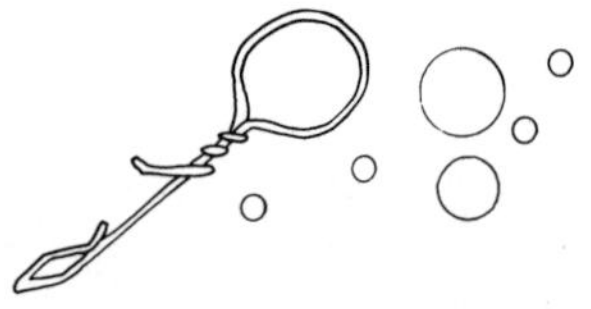		Length
• Brainstorm how to make bubble solution with the class. Let the children experiment to find the best type of solution. They share the best ratios of water to detergent.	Questioning Predicting Experimenting Recording Deciding what is 'best' Explaining Justifying	Ratio of numbers Measurement of volume Recording ratios Recording measurement
• At each table set up containers with water and detergent and with materials including string, scissors, wire, straws, strips of plastic, empty containers to make up their own.		

ACTIVITIES/IDEAS	PROCESSES	FACTS/SKILLS/CONCEPTS
• Children then experiment in making bubbles. Encourage them to ask questions: What is the biggest bubble you can make? What is the smallest bubble you can make? What is the oddest shaped bubble you can make? Can you join two bubbles together? What is the longest it stays as a bubble? What is the furthest it can travel?	Classifying Estimating Comparing Recording Explaining Justifying findings Interpreting data	How to measure things Counting Measurement of size, distance, time Using stop watches or other ways of measuring time
• Once children have completed experiments, discuss findings. These are recorded by the teacher on a sheet of paper titled **What we found out about bubbles**.	Sharing	

7—How can we save water at our school?

ACTIVITIES/IDEAS	PROCESSES	FACTS/SKILLS/CONCEPTS
• Make a list of all possible uses of water. Draw on the children's own experiences but try to extend their ideas beyond the obvious to include less usual areas like paper making or leisure.	Identifying Classifying Estimating	Estimating amounts of liquid Capacity Volume
• Children then sort these into different categories, e.g. cleaning, drinking, heating, pets, leisure etc.	Sorting Classifying	
• Children group themselves according to the category they would most like to work on.	Cooperating	
• Each group is then given the task of first estimating the amount of water consumed per day, then actually testing this estimation. This could be achieved through surveys, discussions with other children and teachers, or setting up a test situation.	Estimating Surveying Collecting data Recording data Explaining their methods	Capacity How to measure amounts of water Calculations on measurements Totals

ACTIVITIES/IDEAS	PROCESSES	FACTS/SKILLS/CONCEPTS
• Once the information has been collected, each group presents their data to the class. This may be done in a variety of ways, e.g. graphs, diagrams, reports etc. It is important that each group shares not only the information they have found, but how this information was gathered.	Presenting Sharing Justifying	Visual representation Using graphs and diagrams Methods of measuring
• The results are then combined to give the whole picture and the data is presented on a graph.	Presenting Representing	Calculation and totals Using graphs Using a calculator
• In groups, children discuss this graph and come up with suggestions on how water can best be saved at the school.	Interpreting graphs Concluding Justifying	Using graphs
• Each group's ideas are collated and a final report is made with a list of recommendations. These could be presented at school assembly or to the principal.	Reporting and presenting data	

8—Building a model of a zoo

ACTIVITIES/IDEAS	PROCESSES	FACTS/SKILLS/CONCEPTS
• Brainstorm all the factors to be considered in building a model of a zoo, e.g. size of enclosures, size of fences, which animals to include, walkways, materials required, organisational details, scale of the zoo etc. These are listed by the teacher on a large sheet of paper or the chalkboard.	Identifying Classifying factors Classifying materials Recording	Concepts of length, area, volume, scale Total amounts of materials needed Measurement and operations on measures
• Children then group themselves into fours and each group decides which animals they would be interested in working on.	Deciding Cooperating	

ACTIVITIES/IDEAS	PROCESSES	FACTS/SKILLS/CONCEPTS
• Each group presents its list and a master list is drawn up showing which group is working on which animals.	Classifying	
• Visit the zoo and get the children to look at all the factors for consideration which were listed for the particular animals they decided to work on.	Identifying Observing animal enclosures	Estimating size Measuring length, area, volume Recording measurements
• After zoo excursion each group discusses factors and comes up with a plan for their particular part of the zoo. These are shared with the other groups and an overall plan of the zoo is drawn up.	Designing Planning Sharing Working together	Diagrams and plans Scale Measurement using scale Working out scale Four operations
• Provide each group with a large sheet of cardboard and various materials for constructing enclosures and animals, e.g. clay, paint, cardboard, scissors, colored paper, markers, wire, beads etc.	Constructing and making Cooperating	Accurate measuring Recording as whole numbers and decimals
• Once all groups have completed their part of the zoo, join these together to form the whole zoo.	Sharing	
• When the zoo is complete, brainstorm with the children the various problems/questions associated with the zoo: e.g. If we were to build a fence around the zoo, how long would this need to be? How many ways can the animals in the zoo be grouped? If each animal requires three litres of water per day, how much water do we need each week? How much and what kind of food do we need for our zoo? If we charge $5 admittance to the zoo and 200 people come each day, how much money will we get per week? Will this cover the food expenses for the animals?	Reflecting Sharing Discussing Interpreting Relating Extrapolating—working out further answers from the data collected Thinking carefully and logically	Calculations based on measurement plans and scale Totals Averages Money Time Weight Using a calculator

Teacher's planning sheet for whole grade explorations

TOPIC: ____________________ DATE: ____________

ACTIVITIES/IDEAS	PROCESSES	FACTS/SKILLS/CONCEPTS

Part 2 (3 weeks)—
individual/small group exploration

Aims

- To develop and extend the children's understandings of mathematical facts, skills and concepts.
- To encourage children to use a variety of processes when exploring areas of interest.
- To encourage children to become independent learners and thinkers.
- To encourage children to develop personal qualities which will support and extend their learning.
- To demonstrate specific skills to children in need.

Getting started

Getting children started on their own explorations is a much more difficult task than introducing the grade to whole class explorations. An effective way to begin this section is to continue your usual program with the majority of the class and get one group of children going on their own explorations. Select children who are already independent learners and who will adopt the approach quickly and easily. Work with this group of children until both you and the children feel confident about the approach—this may take the best part of a week. As you work with this group you will find that other children are very curious and will want to participate too. Once you have one group started and are feeling more familiar with the processes involved, you will be able to introduce a second group to the program. The first group of children will be able to help the others who are ready to start their own explorations.

Part two of the program consists of four tasks—children will initially need a great deal of support in all of these areas:

1 Selecting a topic
Many children will have difficulty in selecting a topic—initially we referred children to a list of measurement areas and suggested they make their selection from these. This resulted in children choosing to explore length, weight or money—concepts that they readily associated with maths and felt secure with. We also felt secure with this as it was not so far removed from what we had traditionally practised. Once children become confident with their own explorations they will begin to explore maths in ways which make sense to them rather than exploring concepts in isolation.

2 Completing a project plan
This is a very important part of the approach which ensures that children are specifically focused in their work. It also ensures that children are engaged in exploring new ideas and not just regurgitating known facts.

3 Collecting, processing and interpreting information
If your children are not familiar with research skills you will need to build this into your program in a major way. This is an excellent opportunity for developing language skills and concepts through the maths curriculum.

4 Presenting information
If your children are familiar with book making they will probably choose to present their maths projects in this format. Allow them to use these skills but after the first project has been completed discuss alternative ways of presenting information.

Give children a rough guideline for working on these tasks over the three week period, e.g.

Week 1—selecting a group and a topic
—completing a project plan
—beginning to explore the topic

Week 2—completing collection, processing and interpreting of information

Week 3—organisation of information for class presentation
—presenting information.

The first three days of this section can be very demanding for the teacher as the children are all at different stages in terms of their readiness to begin their projects. The children need to be supported in their choice of topic, identification of specific areas to explore, and location of resources.

The topics for study in this section are chosen by the children with the support and assistance of their peers and the teacher—they are therefore based on the children's interests.

A list of topics is provided here to support you and your class in individual or small group explorations. They are only suggestions to give you and the children a starting point for their projects. Once the children become familiar with the program and begin to think independently they will produce their own topics. The topics have been grouped into common themes to make them easier for you and the children to use.

Building and constructing

1. Make knives, forks and spoons for the other children in your grade.
2. Plan and make stairs for the stage in your school hall—you will need to look at shape, size and strength.
3. Plan and make a budgie cage.
4. Design and build a device for measuring time—it could be based on sand, sun, water, beans, wind etc.
5. Design and build a car which can move two meters.
6. Design and build a bridge out of paper that will span different distances.
7. Design and build a bridge out of paper that will support a brick for thirty seconds.
8. Design a scale model of your bedroom/house.
9. Design and build a cubby house—how many people will it hold?
10. Design and construct a miniature city.

Ourselves

1 How many breaths would use up all the air in our classroom? How long would this take to occur?
2 Is it true that right-handed people have bigger left feet?
3 How much do the people in your grade weigh altogether? How much do all the people in the school weigh?
4 Design and make a device to lift a child in the class—how high and for how long?
5 How many children would it take to reach the top of the school building?
6 How many hairs are there on your head?
7 How long would an ant take to walk around you? Is this the same for all people in your grade.
8 How old are you exactly?
9 How much are you growing each day?
10 How much money does it take to keep you for a week?
11 How much money does it take to keep your family for a week?
12 Make a birthday chart. Who is the oldest/youngest? Is the oldest the tallest? How old were most people when they started school? What is the total age of the class? Compare this with other classes.
13 Does everyone in the grade have the same pulse rate?

Machines and motion

1 Find out all you can about bikes—gears, wheels, speed etc. Do big bikes move faster than small ones? How far does a bike travel in one turn of a pedal?
2 Find out all you can about paper airplanes. What is the farthest you can make one fly? What effect does the wing span, shape, size have on the distance travelled?
3 How many times does a ball bounce before it stops? Does it depend on the size of ball, height dropped from, what it is made of, surface it bounces on?
4 Find out about cars—speed, capacity, weight, fuel consumption, size, shape etc.
5 Find out all you can about parachutes—shapes, design, distance, weight, speed etc.
6 How many different ways are there of getting from home to school? Design a map to show each route and the time it takes.
7 Find out what you can about TV. How does it work? How much time is spent on advertisements (per day or per hour)? How much TV does the class watch per day? You could use graphs here.
8 How many cars pass by your school per day?
9 How many trucks pass by your school per hour?
10 How many different things can you do in five minutes?

Food

1. How much food do you eat—day, month, year? Which type of food do you eat the most?
2. Make a cake that is big enough for the whole class/school.
3. Plan a food stall to raise money for something your class/school needs.
4. Choose a pet. How much will it cost you to feed it each year?
5. How many bean plants are needed to fill a can of baked beans?
6. Make a book of your favourite recipes.
7. Compare the amounts of different foods you get that weigh 50 grams. How many noodles equal 50 grams of rice?
8. Plan a lunch for the whole grade to eat.
9. How much Vegemite is consumed daily in your school?
10. What happens to different foods when they are cooked? e.g. How much does rice swell?

Plants and animals

1. Find out all you can about trees around your school—types, heights, ages, widths, shapes—number of branches, leaves, inhabitants.
2. Find out all you can about animals—life-span, fastest, slowest, tallest, smallest, lightest, heaviest, strongest—where they live, what they eat, how much they eat.
3. Make a food chain of the animals around the school.
4. Find out all you can about planting and growing seeds. Experiment with different amounts of light, water, warmth and conversation.
5. What animals can you run faster than?
6. How long does it take a snail to move one metre?
7. How long does it take a caterpillar to eat three leaves?
8. Construct an ant farm and find out how much an ant eats each week.
9. Find out all you can about planting bulbs.
10. Make a survey about the different pets people in your grade have.

General

1. Find out all you can about shadows.
2. What supplies are needed for your grade each year—amounts of pencils, paper, Textas, books, paint etc?
3. You have just won $1 000 000. Write down how you will spend it—you may find shopping catalogues will help you.
4. Design your own secret letter code using symbols or sounds.

5 Design your own number system. How does it compare to ours?
6 Design and make a device for sending messages from one part of the school to another.
7 Make a chart of your day. How long do you spend eating, sleeping, talking, playing, reading etc?
8 Using the Guinness Book of Records and string, measure out some of the longest, shortest, or widest things in the world.
9 Make clothing for the class out of newspaper.
10 Find out all you can about our solar system, e.g. stars, distance between planets, size of planets, temperatures, light years etc.
11 Find out all you can about tides and the moon. How big is the moon?
12 Find out all you can about bubbles.

Example of a unit

Week 1— *TOPIC SELECTION*

Many children have chosen to explore concepts and areas of knowledge that were suggested by the whole grade exploration. We read through the list, compiled at the end of Part 1, about who was doing what and children elaborated on what they were intending to explore.

Ideas to assist topic selection

- Display a list showing
  - projects that children have already selected;
  - ideas for projects.
- Display an on-going list of projects done by children.
- Make a folder and keep a list of project ideas in them. Teachers and children can add to these folders.
- Have individual or small group conferences to brainstorm ideas. Talk to the children about what is happening in their lives.

Considerations

- Ensure that children select a topic that will maintain their interest for three weeks.
- Some children will need a great deal of teacher support in selecting a topic.

- Many children will choose to continue to work on issues that they were exploring in Part one because their interest has been stimulated and they feel comfortable and secure with this particular issue.

Completing a project plan

Once children have selected a topic they need to focus their investigations. An effective way to do this is to have children complete a project plan.

Step 1 Children list everything they know about the topic, then share their list with others in their group.

We included this step because initially the children's completed projects would often comprise a published form of what they already knew about a topic rather than documentation of new understandings they had developed. It also helped them to identify a specific focus for their explorations.

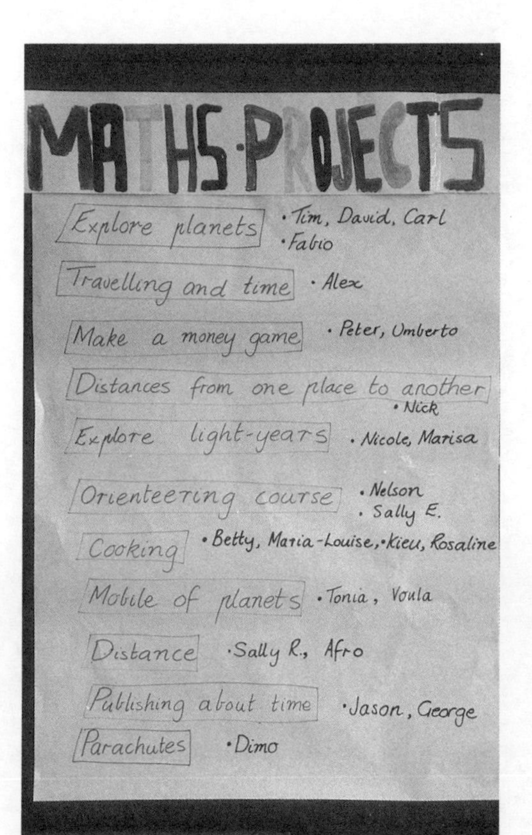

Step 2 Children conference with group members in order to work out what they don't know about the topic.

We demonstrated this procedure to the children in the following way. We decided to explore the topic of parachutes, as we had been playing with one in our sports sessions. We wrote down everything we knew about parachutes and then had a conference with the whole grade. The children told us everything they thought we didn't know about parachutes and we added comments about these areas to our draft. We then had a list of starting points for our explorations.

An example of a project plan about planets.

PROJECT PLAN

Names David
Tim
Carl

1. Topic

Planets

2. Everything I know (attached)

3. What I don't know

Age of solar system?
Details about planets?
solar system (Others)?
Life on other planets?

4. What I want to find out

Have the planets moved? Whats on planets? How big are the planets?

Approved
Date 15/11/88

What I know about planets

Jupitar is the biggest planet in our solar system.
There are 9 planets in our (solar system) (others?), they are (Age of solar system)
Earth, Jupitar, Mars, Venus, Mercury, saturn, Uraunas, Neptane
& pluto. Saturn has a ring of gases around it.
Uranus has 4 moons, Jupitar has 4, Earth has 1 (Details about planets)
Neptune has 1 as well. Pluto is the futherest from (Life on other planets)
the sun. The sun is a star. Mercury is the
closest to the sun. Venus is the hottest in our
solar system its temp 427°C 800°F. Pluto is the coldest
Planet its temp -184°C -300°F ? ? (Have Moved?) (What's on Planets) (How Big)

Step 3 Children list everything they don't know on their project plan.

Step 4 Children select issues from their list of 'what we don't know' which they would like to explore.

Step 5 Children arrange a conference with the teacher in order to discuss their groups' intentions. Children are asked to justify the project in terms of its maths content. The teacher approves the plan and ensures that the group has appropriate resources to begin their investigation.

Beginning to collect information

Resources—as soon as topics are selected both teacher and children must gather relevant resources from a variety of sources:
- school library
- regional library
- science room
- home
- institutions/groups
- maths resource area

- Teachers need to discuss the variety of sources of information and how students can utilise them.
- Teachers need to model how information can be taken from a pamphlet, book etc and used for one's own purposes.
- Projects can take a variety of forms:
  - constructing a model
  - making a cake
  - preparing an orienteering course
  - weighing everyone in the grade

Danny decided to measure the perimeter of the room although he didn't seem to have much idea of what perimeter was. I suggested he draw a diagram of the room but he really didn't see a need for it. He got a trundle wheel and began to measure. He later came to me to show me how he'd measured the two parts of the room—it added up to exactly the entire length. He was quite impressed with his discovery but was very frustrated with his inability to find the right words to explain it.

George decided to weigh everyone again (it was done by Sally in February) and to see how much weight we'd gained and who'd gained the most—he used Sally's data from February.

Week 2— COMPLETING INFORMATION COLLECTION

All children are now working on their projects. Tim, Carl and David are very involved with their explorations about planets. Betty, Kieu and Rosaline are enthusiastic about their cooking but are needing constant guidance and support, e.g. today I had to explain how many grams (and ounces too) there are in a teaspoon. Danny is working particularly well now that he's found an interest. Umberto and Peter appear to be getting very little out of making a game—they are not particularly interested in what they've chosen to do and it shows.

We talked about various ways of presenting information: Tim, Carl and David decided they'd write it up in their personal maths folder because that's the quickest way—they want to spend as much time as possible in exploring.

I asked them to justify the maths project from a maths point of view—they did it poorly—as a class we discussed the project and the children offered suggestions.

Considerations

- Children will be at different stages of involvement in their projects and will need varying amounts of support and direction from the teacher.
- Hold individual and small group conferences for those who need them.
- Hold scheduled meetings for all children.
- Support the children's learning by sharing a continued interest in their projects and an awareness of where they are with it.
- Extend children's learning by posing appropriate questions.
- Provide clinics based on identified needs.
- Encourage children to work cooperatively in solving their problems.
- Encourage the children's sense of a community of learners.
- Encourage children to share their methods of working on their projects.
- Demonstrate ways of recording findings.
- Allow children to record, process, interpret and present their findings in ways that are appropriate for them:
  - demonstrate how to represent information on diagrams, tables or graphs;
  - demonstrate how to process data, working out totals, averages and differences;
  - demonstrate how to interpret results, looking for relationships or patterns, drawing out generalisations and supporting hypotheses.
- Ensure that children justify their projects in terms of how it is helping them with maths—this makes them very aware of the maths in their world and also helps to direct their explorations.

Week 3—
PRESENTING THE INFORMATION

David, Tim and Carl are still collecting information about planets—they have decided to record their findings in an exercise book as this will be quick, easy and allow them more time to continue their research.

We've eaten Betty and Kien and Rosalind's cake—it was delicious. They're busy writing up the procedure in a recipe book they have now decided to write.

Most children are presenting their information on charts, one group has produced a board game and another is making a book about length.

Jason and Nick's book about length.

Length is how long something is you can measure length with cm, metres and kilometres. You can use a ruler, a tape measure a trundle wheel, feet, hands, and string.

Made in Australia Rulex-TrueLine

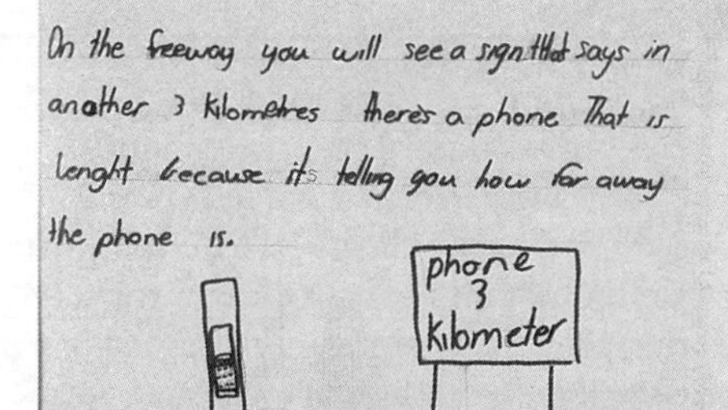

We went around the grade and found out how has the longest of everything the longest leg is Nelson 98cm long. The Longest foot is David 31cm Long

Now we are going to mesare things in our class room door is 210cm Hight. The Blackboard is 643cm long and our classroom is 15.00 metres long, the Hallway is 2156cm. The table is 1.7cm long, Chadwick is 27cm Hight.

About the AUTHORS

Hi My name is Jason and I live 17 spring st Coburg My Hobbies are football, Soccer, Cricket. I am 10 years old. I am in grade 5 I was Born on the 1/2/78 That's all For now "BYE"

Hi My name is Nick I live at 29 queen st east. Brunswick My Hobbies are Football, soccer, and Publishing, storys. I am 12 years old I was born in greece thats all for now. BYE

Considerations

- Discuss the purpose of recording findings
- Encourage children to record their findings in ways that make sense to them
- Demonstrate ways of recording data

> The children shared their projects today . . . it was great! We have a new method for sharing—we used to ask each group to do a 'show and tell' of their project—the children decided this was boring and took too long—it did too! They suggested that we put all the projects together on a table and then spend the morning reading each others—we built a little structure into this by giving the children a sheet with specific headings—it worked extremely well. Children were most professional in the way they managed the session—we finished by collating individual 'share-time' sheets onto a class list which reflected how we felt about the projects generally.

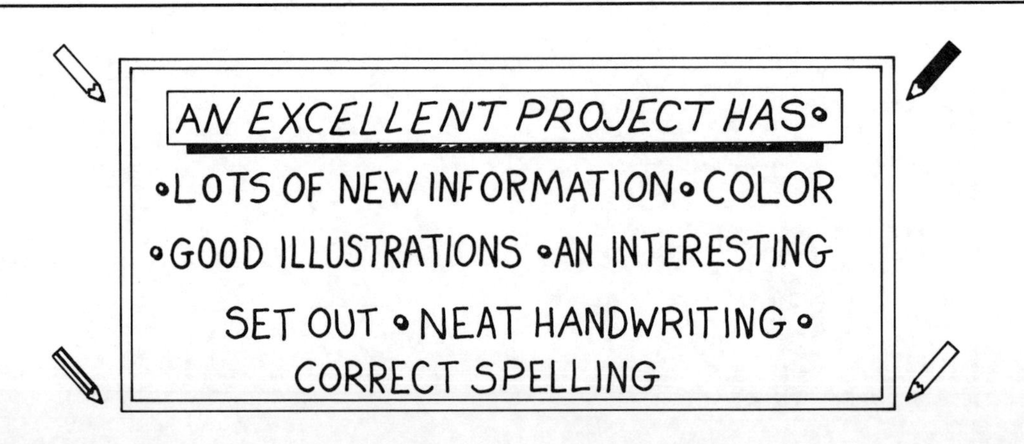

Considerations

- Allow time for children to share and celebrate their projects with others in the grade.
- Continually evaluate the effectiveness of classroom strategies and allow children to suggest alternative strategies.
- Demonstrate written and oral responses to projects.
- Reflect on the achievements of the children as a whole and make a chart which celebrates these but also directs children to issues that need to be focused on next time.

Part 3 (one week)—Investigations

The intention of this part of the program is to provide children with learning experiences that are significantly different from those encountered in the first two parts of the program, in that they are directed at maths for maths sake—the abstract as against the applied side of the subject. The activities in this section also immerse children in mathematics. The focus is to enable children to develop the mathematical processes that may not have occurred in parts 1 and 2.

There are several kinds of activities that can be used to help children develop the ability to use mathematical processes—the ones described here are investigations and *Logo*. Investigations are activities that develop into a diverging sequence of questions and problems. They do not have one right answer—different children follow different paths, each asking their own questions and making their own discoveries. Unlike previous sections, the children are not required to chart their activities in detail. An example of one of these activities is 'Squares', which is discussed in detail on page 45. The second activity area is *Logo*, a computer language where children explore mathematical ideas in a similar manner to investigations. There is no space in this book to adequately describe how to use *Logo* with children. However, many accounts have been written about children exploring mathematics through *Logo* and these are referred to in the bibliography.

Aims

- To develop children's ability to use mathematical processes, in particular their ability to think divergently, reflect, relate, generalise, specialise, justify their results and communicate them.
- To develop children's mathematical facts, skills, and concepts, in particular, number facts and skills, spatial relations, and visual representations.

- To develop children's personal qualities of perseverence, concentration, cooperation and attitude.

Getting started

Four stages can be identified in working with investigations:
1 *Doing*
2 *Reflecting*
3 *Pursuing*
4 *Sharing*

Children will differ in the amount of time that they spend on each of these stages. Some children will move on to the reflecting stage very quickly, while others will spend much more time 'doing'. Teachers need to encourage children to move on through the stages so that eventually they learn to generalise about strategies.

Selecting a topic—Squares
The first time we used investigations with our class we introduced a strategy game called Squares. We had tried it ourselves and believed that it would challenge and interest the children. A further collection of investigational activities is provided at the end of this section and sources of ideas are included in the bibliography at the end of the book to help you add to the list.

STAGE 1 - DOING

We briefly explained the game to the children and they played it. Many children struggled with the game and just kept playing in the hope that they'd gain some insight into how to win all the time—Betty and Rosalind were among these. They recorded the games in their own ways. George started to mark the board on paper, drawing possible patterns and trying them out.

Considerations

- The children in your class may need help with getting started on the investigation, but once they have begun they become very involved in it and quickly find ways of keeping records of their work. They often get help from each other. The teacher should only help when the children are getting frustrated.

STAGE 2 – REFLECTING

The children began to *hypothesise* about winning: 'Does the starter always win?' 'Does it matter where you start?' 'Are some squares good and some bad?'

Fabio tried to simplify the game to a more manageable situation by reducing the size of the game board.

On the basis of their records the children predicted who would win the next game and generalised about winning strategies. Carl was one of the first to discover what he felt was a fool-proof winning strategy. He thought some of the squares were good and he would win from them. Other squares always led to him losing, so he had to avoid them. The other children tried to learn from him but could not follow his explanation.

Considerations

- This is a vital part of the activity, because this is where children extend their ability to use mathematical processes. Armed with their results, the children need to be encouraged to stand back and *think*, as they will often continue to work on the investigation with little or no reflection. They need to look for *patterns and relationships*, *predict* their next results and *test* their predictions by trying a *special* case. It is important that they make *generalisations* about their results, and *question* and *justify* their findings.

STAGE 3 – PURSUING

At this stage the children are very confident and know a lot about the game. We encouraged them to continue exploring by changing some of the rules, e.g. changing the size of the board to a 4 x 4 square. Once Nelson had discovered a winning strategy he extended the board to 5 x 6, and tried his strategy out again. Some children preferred to try their own investigation or play a maths game instead of pursuing the 'squares'.

Considerations

- This stage is about asking questions that open out the investigation. Useful questions are 'What if something were changed?' or 'What if we left something out?' or 'What if it were bigger?'. Children need a lot of help initially with finding ways to open out their investigations.

STAGE 4 – SHARING

After four sessions the children were ready to share their results. Some of them were keen to do this by playing the game. Others displayed their ideas on paper. The whole class talked about the game and we drew up a list of important strategies, e.g. how to simplify problems when you are stuck and how to record results in the best way.

Considerations

- The children share and *justify* their results. They may have difficulties *explaining* their ideas. Often they are short of words and they need to try and use drawings or graphs to help them *communicate*. They share their ways of solving the problems and these are recorded as part of a class resource of problem-solving approaches.

Activities

A list of investigations has been provided below to support you in the investigations in part 3 of the program. These are intended to be the beginning of your own list of such activities. You are encouraged to extend the list either from ideas brought in by the children or from ideas you find in the bibliography.

Squares

This activity needs a game board (as shown below) and one counter. It is a game for two people and is based on an idea from the National Council of Teachers of Mathematics (USA), 'Student maths notes', May 1987.

Procedure

The first player places the counter on one of the squares on the starting line. The second player then moves the counter either along or down. They cannot move it diagonally, upward or to a previously used square. Player 1 then moves in the same way. Players take turns moving in this way until one player moves into the target area. That player is the winner.

Game Board

Comments

At first the children will simply want to play. After a while they need to be encouraged to stand back and think about what they have been doing—by looking for winning strategies. One way of doing this is to ask them whether the winner is the player who starts. Once they have begun to think about the game they then find questions of their own, e.g. Does it matter which square they choose for the first counter? This game has a lot of possibilities. You need to avoid the children saying they have finished after playing it a few times. Some children will need careful encouragement to really think. Others will work at the ideas for the whole week.

Extensions

1 Change the size of the board. Try smaller or larger boards. Compare results for boards with an odd or even number of

rows. Do the winning strategies apply to all sizes of boards? Are there vital squares or vital moves?

2. Change the shape of the board to a rectangle. Does this make a difference?
3. Change the rules of the game. Allow the children to try and design their own versions.
4. Change the game board to a triangular shape.

What the children can learn

Content

Understanding different types of numbers. Using odd and even numbers. Number patterns. Relating number of squares left in a row or column to moves needed. Types of shapes. Use of shapes and effects of changing shapes.

Processes

Problem-solving strategies. Recording results of playing the game and extracting information from the results. Looking for ways of showing each game graphically and relating the results. Generalising. Setting up hypotheses for winning strategies. Looking for evidence to support hypotheses and then accepting or refining ideas. Justifying conclusions and explaining them to others. Creating new rules and new games. Awareness that thinking about the game can give better game-playing strategies than repeated playing of the game.

Dipping Rhymes

A 'Dipping Rhyme' is one used to choose the person to be 'it' in a game. Some people use one that begins 'One potato, two potato, . . .'. Each time the rhyme ends one person is out, leaving one person at the very end who is 'it'!

Procedure

Write down a rhyme that you use in your school. In groups choose one and decide how you will use it. Try and write this down. Use the rhyme in your group to see who is 'it'. Can you predict beforehand who will be 'it'?

Comments

Children like to use their playground experiences in the classroom and they engage in this activity very readily. There is a tendency for them to use unacceptable rhymes and that must be up to you to control. You will need to encourage them to think about the problem after a few goes and to persevere with it to avoid the 'done it' after five minutes syndrome. It is useful to be ready to ask questions like 'Does the result depend on who starts the rhyme or how long it is?'. For those who are stuck you can suggest using a very short rhyme, one, say, with only three words. Most of them like the activity although it does not produce quick answers. It has an easy entry for the slower children and yet can genuinely stretch the most able. We had a mathematically gifted child who worked on the activity for the whole week and still had more to explore.

Extensions

1. At first let the children find their own rhymes and decide the rules. For example, is 'it' the first person eliminated or the last one? The first case is easier to explore than the second, but the latter has richer possibilities.
2. The children occasionally choose rhymes whose length changes depending on a number inserted by one of them, e.g. 'Little Miss Piggy'. This can make the problem too difficult at first so try to talk the children out of it but allow them to come back to it later.
3. Encourage the children to write about their rhymes and to present illustrated versions of them.
4. Encourage them to represent their results in their own ways. These can be a drawing of a circle or a line, the use of counters or they may describe it or write about it using words or symbols.
5. Change the number of people in the groups. Does this affect their results? Can they predict who will be 'it' for any number of people?
6. Let them change the rhymes. Can they predict the results for any length of rhyme?
7. Let them design their own rhymes.

What the children can learn

Content

They are involved in a great amount of number activities. They count, they represent numbers in different groupings, they use place value, they use the four number operations, and they look for relationships between numbers. They need to represent their ideas using symbols and they can extend the ideas to modular arithmetic.

Processes
Problem-solving techniques trying easier situations using shorter rhymes and fewer people. Looking for patterns and results and generalising from these to more complex situations. Setting up hypotheses and looking for evidence to support their ideas. Refining their ideas in the light of their results and asking their own questions. Presenting their results, convincing others and using them in the playground.

Arithmetrics

The numbers on the sides of the triangle were found by adding the pairs of numbers at each end of the sides. Unfortunately the three numbers in the boxes at the end of each side were written in invisible ink and were lost. Can you find the numbers that were in the boxes?

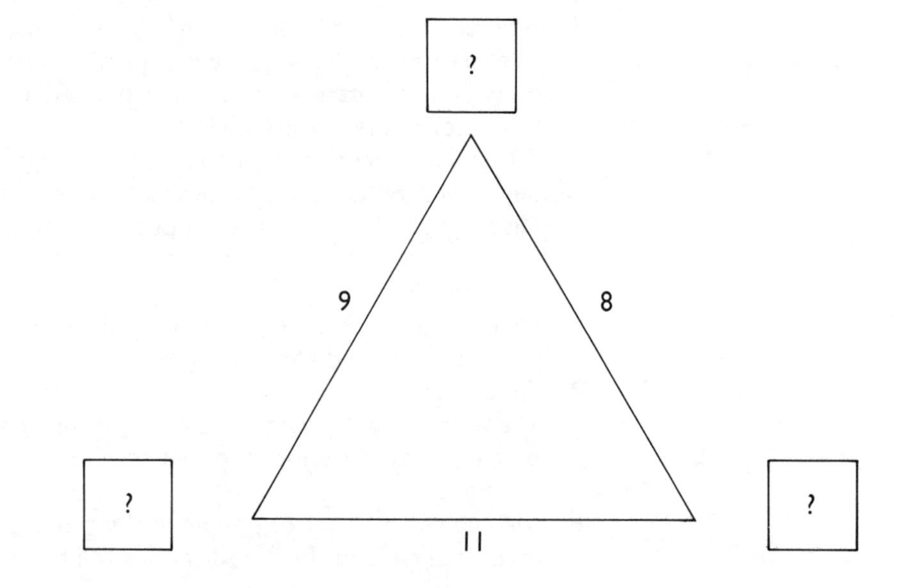

Comments

This is an interesting educational activity, and the children get really involved in searching for the numbers. It has a very easy entry point, and the solution is not hard to find by trial and error, so the children do need encouragement to ask their own questions and to look for extensions (see below).

Extensions

1 Change the numbers.
2 Use other operations like times or difference or average. Subtraction and division are more complicated but they can try them if they want to.

3. Use other types of numbers—decimals, fractions, negatives.
4. Use other shapes.
5. For those who find this activity too difficult, you can give them the 'corner numbers' and let them find the 'sides'. They will find that much easier.
6. The children can create their own 'arithmeshapes' using their own operations.

What the children can learn

Content

Number facts and number operations. They learn about the order of operations, e.g. 3 + 6 = 6 + 3. They learn about the use of symbols to represent numbers—the beginning of algebra, box arithmetic, e.g. ☐ + ☐ = 9.

Processes

Problem-solving strategies. The children use trial and error by trying a few numbers and then getting these guesses closer and closer until all three numbers work. They develop a feel for the size of numbers and the effect of different operations. Their guesses are in fact hypotheses and they learn to choose numbers intelligently based on evidence of earlier trials. They try to generalise their methods and to use unknowns.

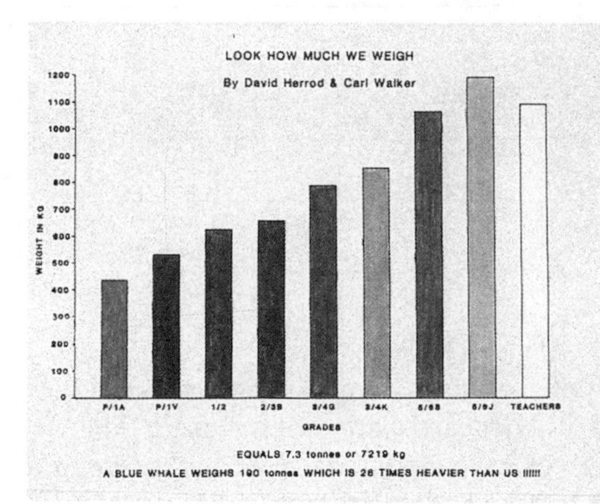

David and Carl weighed the entire school population to see how heavy we were.

Peter and Fabio made a box containing the longest things in the world with the aid of the *Guinness Book of Records*. Measuring out each object with string, they attached a picture of the object with relevant information about it to the end of the string. They are pictured showing the widest wingspan of a bird ever recorded.

Make the Most Game

The game needs a board as shown below and a set of playing cards with the digits 1 to 9 on them, placed face down next to the board.

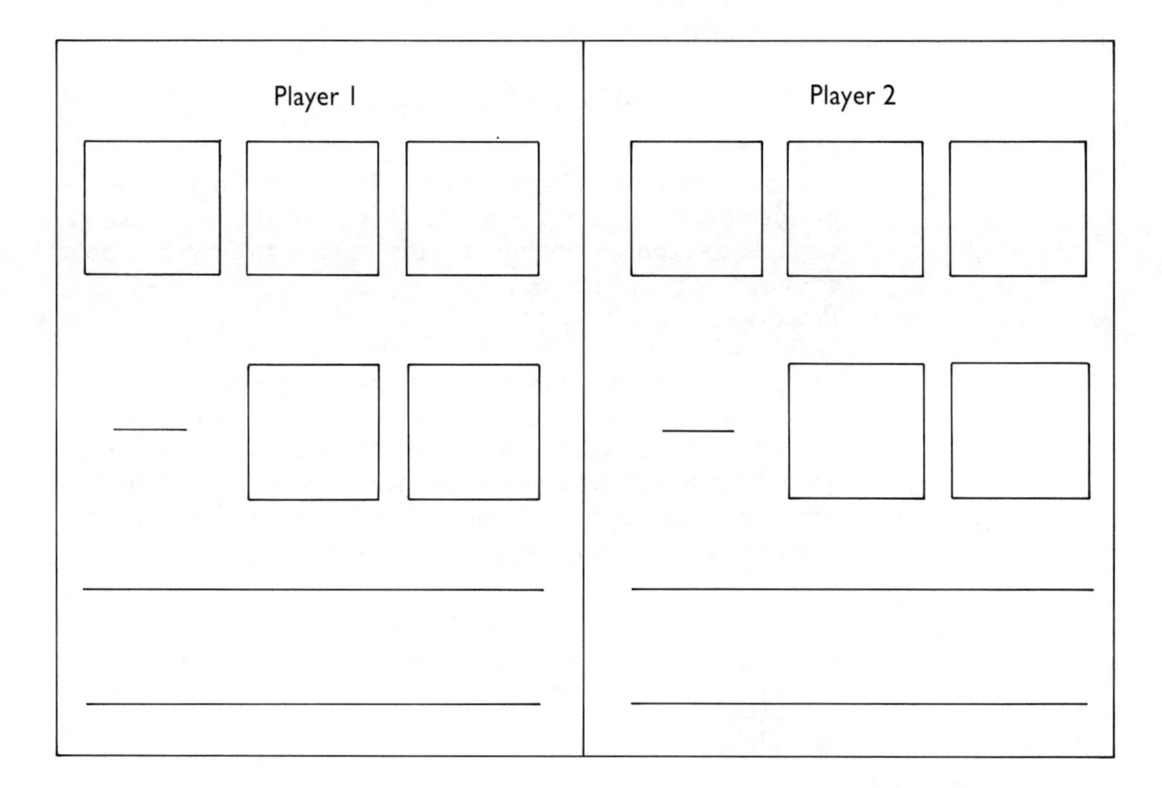

Procedure

Taking turns each player takes a card and marks the digit from the card on their *own* board. The cards are not re-used. This is continued until all the squares have digits. The subtraction is then done. The winner is the player with the largest answer.

Comments

This is a closed activity with very clear educational goals. It is designed to build children's basic number skills and also their awareness of number. The children enjoy the game and some have found their own ways of opening the activity. It is well worth encouraging them to look closely at the possibilities listed below and even invent their own. For those children with less number skills the board can be changed to use two digit numbers on the top line and one on the bottom. To save arguments, a calculator is a useful arbitrator.

Extensions

1. Change the board to use two and four digit numbers.
2. The game can be played cooperatively with the children trying to make the largest number they can.
3. Change the rules to allow them to insert their digits on each other's board. This is a very stimulating version.
4. Change the end of the game, so the winner is the one with the smallest total.
5. Use other operations—addition, multiplication, difference, average and even division.
6. Change the rules to allow cards to be returned to the pack and shuffled.
7. Give the board decimal points to allow tenths, hundredths etc. to be used.
8. Make the board longer to allow addition of three or more numbers.

What the children can learn

Content
Number facts and skills with the four basic operations on whole numbers and decimals. Understanding place value and the four operations. Learning about probability and chance.
Processes
Encouraging a feeling for number. Estimation and an awareness of what each of the operations does to numbers. The effect of changing digits on the answer to sums. Generalising from patterns in the games played to build up winning strategies. Decision making, e.g. Is '5' a big or small digit?

Frogs

Three green frogs are sitting on lily pads, one behind the other. In front of them is an empty pad and beyond that are three brown frogs facing them on three more pads in a line. The frogs can only move forwards and can either slide onto an empty lily pad or hop over another frog onto a pad.

Can you move the green frogs to the brown frogs' lily pads and the brown ones to the green frogs' pads?

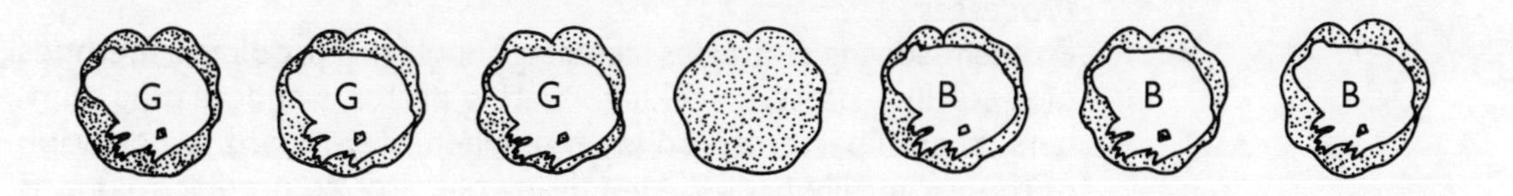

Comments

The best way to start this problem is to put out seven chairs and get six children to act the part of the frogs in front of the whole class. The session will get fairly lively as all will want to contribute. At this point it is important that they all have a go at it in groups. If chairs and space are limited then use counters, but there are advantages in using the children themselves. The problem is easy to understand and start and yet opens out very quickly into many possible routes. At the start some children will quickly claim to have a solution. If so, ask them to repeat it. Problems of reproducing their solution lead the children to develop fascinating systems of recording and explaining. If some get stuck it is worth suggesting simplifying the problem to one or two frogs on each side and to look for patterns in the position of the frogs when they do get stuck. Space needs to be provided for display of solutions and time needs to be allocated to allow some groups to explore many of the possibilities.

Extensions

1. Encourage the children to find the least number of moves to solve the problem.
2. Change the number of frogs to one or two on each side. Then change them to more than three. From the patterns in their results get them to predict the number of moves for any number of frogs.
3. Encourage the children to record their moves in their own way.
4. Let them change the rules to allow different numbers of frogs on each side, or more than one vacant pad, or different moves, e.g. backwards.
5. Encourage them to ask their own questions and look for patterns in their results.

What the children can learn

Content
Looking for number patterns, odds and evens, using number facts and operations. Recording results graphically.

Processes
Problem-solving strategies including simplifying problems, methods of recording, pattern seeking, relating patterns and relating numbers. Spacial patterns also emerge when they record the position of the vacant lily pads. Generalising patterns to predict solutions for different numbers of frogs. Justifying results and explaining solutions.

The Merry-Go-Round

We are going to make a chain of numbers using the following rules. Choose any number between 1 and 39, e.g. choose **27**. Now change it in this strange way:

Take the units digit, the **7**, and multiply it by 4, i.e. 7 x 4 = 28.

Take the tens digit, the **2** and add it on to the 28, i.e. 28 + 2 gives the new number **30**. So **27** becomes **30**.

Now do the same to the new number **30**. **30** becomes 0 x 4 = 0, and adding the 3 gives the new number **3**. Continuing this way, **3** becomes 3 x 4 = 12, adding the tens which is 0 gives the next new number **12**. We therefore have the start of a chain of numbers:

27 → 30 → 3 → 12?

What happens next? Why is it called 'The Merry-Go-Round'?

Comments

The rules seem a little complicated at first but once explained the children find it easy to start. It is also easy to work at it for a long time without stopping to think about what is happening. Some of them work systematically through all the numbers between 1 and 39 enjoying the repetition of the calculations without noticing that once a number has appeared in a chain it is not necessary to look at it again. This seems to be an important pattern to notice and so you may need to encourage them to see it by getting them to discuss and explain their ideas. It is also important to let them devise their own ways of recording their work. For some groups of children a calculator is vital, others find it slows them down too much and so use it infrequently. Results do arise fairly quickly at first and the children need to be encouraged to ask their own questions and to try other possibilities.

Extensions

1 Look for patterns in the numbers that do not change.
2 Find the length of chains and the number of chains.
3 Look at numbers beyond 39.
4 Try other numbers, e.g. negative numbers.
5 Change the rules, e.g. multiply units by 2 and add the tens.
6 Allow different operations, e.g. subtract the tens.

What the children can learn

Content

Familiarity and practice in handling numbers. Number skills and operations. Number facts and tables. Increased awareness of place value. Types of numbers—primes, odds and evens, multiples and factors.

Processes

Developing problem-solving strategies—systematic, approximations and improvement, looking for patterns, standing back and thinking about results. Asking their own questions like 'Why are there only 9 chains?' or 'Why is 13 in a chain of its own?' Given that 13 and 26 are in chains on their own, predicting what will happen to 39 or later to 52, 65, or 78. Explaining and justifying results, conjectures and conclusions.

A Dotty World

We are going to explore a world of dots. All the houses in the world are drawn on dotty paper. The plan of one of the houses is shown here:

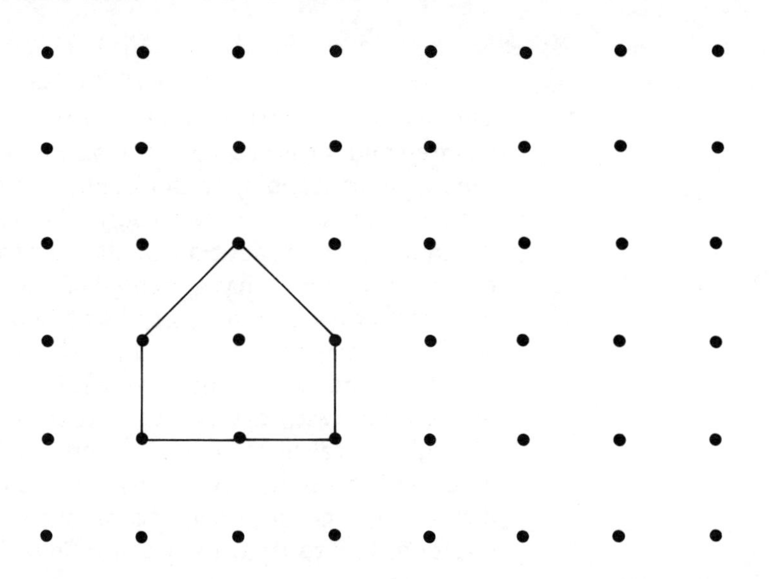

The walls of the house join up six dots. There is one dot inside and it has an area of three squares. 'Dotty World' children like houses with only one dot inside them. Can you design others? What can you find out about 'Dotty World' houses?

Comments

An easy entry to this very open problem which has some compact results. There are relationships between the number of dots on the walls, the number inside and the area. The children do need help understanding plans, help with counting the dots on the walls (concept of perimeter), and some need to understand area and how to measure it. They very quickly design complicated plans and then find relationships difficult to see. After a while you need to suggest a simpler, systematic approach where the houses are steadily made bigger or smaller and the results kept, preferably in a table. Display of their designs helps the sharing of ideas.

Extensions

1 Encourage the children to keep the houses simple, with only one dot inside.
2 Allow them to try houses with two dots inside.
3 Encourage them to have any number of dots inside, even 0.
4 Vary the dots inside but keep the area or perimeter fixed.
5 Design their own world.

What the children can learn

Content

Concepts of area and perimeter. Measurement of area. When looking for patterns they use number facts, tables and the four operations. The use of symbols to show relationships, and aspects of algebra. Ideas of plans and spatial relations.

Processes

Problem-solving strategies, being systematic and looking for patterns and relationships in simpler cases. Methods of recording results on tables. Methods of showing relationships and ideas and explaining them. Generalising from particular cases to general results.

A chart showing the oldest in the grade to the youngest, with questions for the reader to answer.

A collection of books published for different explorations.

Ring of Beads

Using three black beads and two white beads I can make this ring. How many different rings can you make using the same beads?

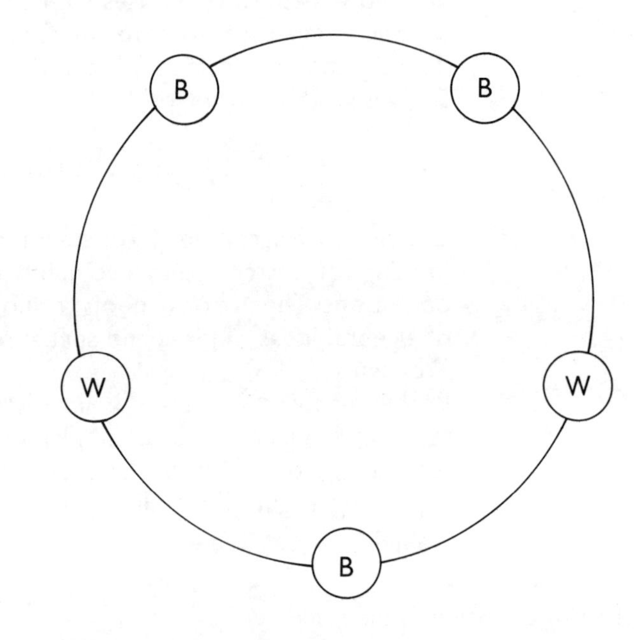

Comments

Given some beads and threading strings, the children find this problem easy to start. They have to make decisions to determine whether two rings are different. Ones that have the same arrangement but are in a different position are usually regarded as the same ring. Once they have looked at 3 black and 2 white bead rings they need to be encouraged to vary the situation. Some of the possible variations are listed below. Again, a display of their results and ideas is important as it helps the class share ideas and learning.

Extensions

1. Using five beads, vary the numbers of each colour.
2. Vary the number of beads used.
3. Vary the number of colours used.
4. Change the shape of the jewellery to allow rows of beads or figures of eight etc.

What the children can learn

Content

Using counting to learn about combinations. Number patterns. Spatial relations when using rotations and reflections to decide which arrangements of beads are distinct.

Processes
Systematic ways of approaching problems and recording results. Looking for patterns and relationships. Generalising results. Predicting specific results for particular numbers of beads from general ones.

Escape from Numberland Prison

Numbers are held in prison unless they can change themselves into the number one. They are only allowed to change themselves using these rules:

If they are even then they can halve themselves.

If they are odd then they multiply themselves by 3 and add 1.

If we try **5**, it changes like this. **5** is an odd number so multiply it by 3 and add 1, i.e. 5 x 3 = 15, then 15 + 1 = **16**. **5 → 16**. Now **16** is even and is therefore halved. It becomes **8**. Continuing in this way we can see what happens to **5** in the end:

5 → 16 → 8 → 4 → 2 → 1

So **5** escapes! What can you find out about the unfortunate numbers in this prison?

Comments

The children explore to see whether all numbers can escape. Under these rules all whole numbers do escape. Encourage them to think carefully before trying numbers. After a while they find that the number they are using has been used as part of a previous escape route. Encourage them to record their results carefully.

Extensions

1. Look at the patterns and types of routes the numbers follow.
2. Look at the length of the routes they take.
3. Change the rules used, e.g. if the number is odd, multiply by 5 and subtract 3.
4. Encourage them to make their own rules.

What the children can learn

Content
Use and practice of number facts and skills. A feeling for number and the effect that different operations have on them. Concepts of odd and even, multiples and factors. Methods of recording results and data—tables and graphs. Using data and graphs.

Processes
Problem-solving skills. Seeking patterns. Speculating about results and predicting future results. Finding conclusions and justifying ideas. Explaining and arguing about results.

Towers

We are going to build towers using cubes. I like towers that look like this.

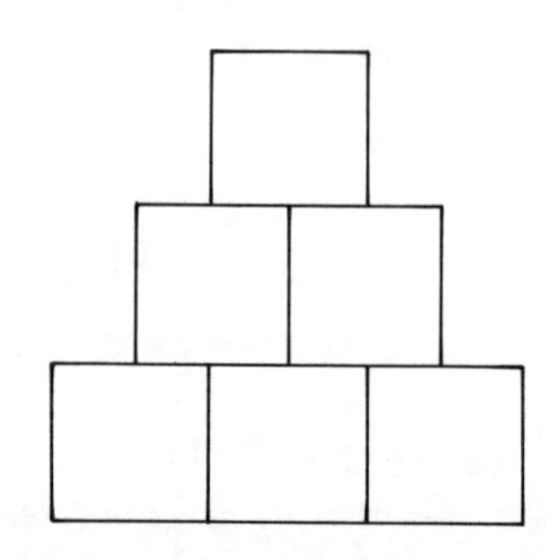

The cubes overlap. We want to make lots of different size towers but do not know how many cubes we will need.

Comments

Many children will need plain cubes to start the activity. It is one that they find easy to get started and more difficult to find questions to pursue later. But encourage them to ask their own questions. The usual one is 'How many do we need to make a tower 5 storeys high?'. Others are 'How many more do we need to make a 2-storey tower into a 6-storey tower?', or 'How many more do we need to double the height of the tower?'.

Extensions

1 The children can make several towers and count the cubes they used. Then, by looking for patterns, they can try to predict the numbers they will need. They can therefore try both smaller towers or taller ones. Encourage them to look for reasons for their patterns.
2 Encourage them to design their own towers—perhaps using 5 on the bottom, then 3 above and 1 on top—to produce their own patterns.
3 They can do the same with three-dimensional towers. These can have different shaped bases. Some can be square based, others triangles etc.
4 They can move away from shapes and explore different sorts of number sequences, e.g. triangular numbers, square numbers, cube numbers etc.

What the children can learn

Content

Skills in the basic operations. Number facts and tables. Ways of recording results. Properties of shapes and ideas of balance and symmetry.

Processes
Number patterns and sequences. Asking their own questions. Identifying relationships. Predicting results and justifying conclusions. Creating their own designs, patterns, and results.

Chess Board

A chess board looks like this

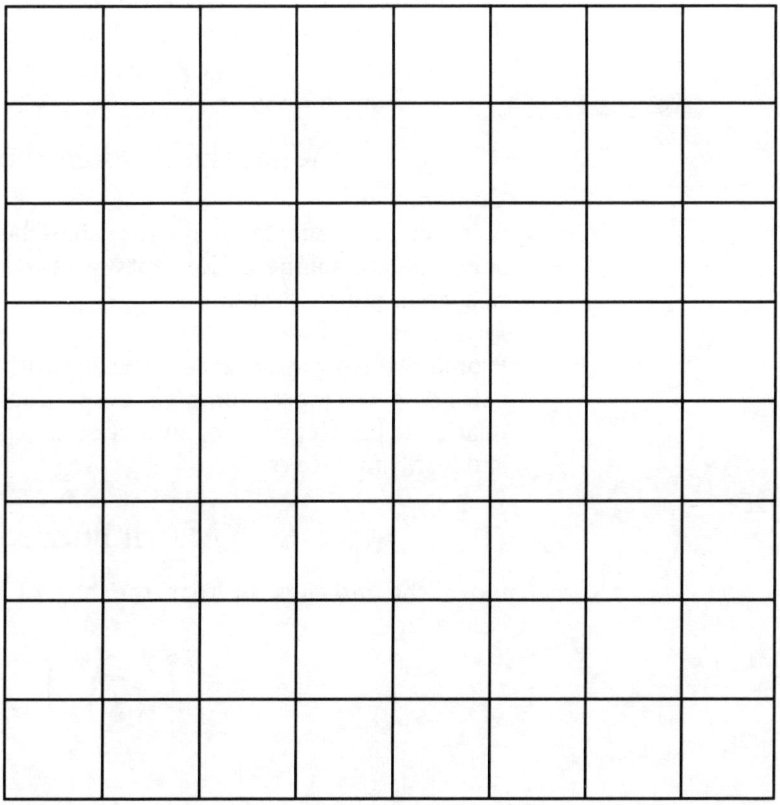

How many squares are there on the board? (There may be different sized squares on the board.)

Comments

The children find the complete board daunting and it is a good idea to encourage them to look at simpler cases. By looking at a one by one board and then a two by two board, they can build up results and look for patterns. They can then generalise their results and use these to predict the special result for the standard chess board.

Extensions

1. A useful case to look at is a three by three board where the children find:
   1 x 3 by 3 squares
   4 x 2 by 2 squares
   9 x 1 by 1 square
   This shows the build up of the patterns of the numbers 1, 4, 9, . . . the square numbers.
2. Explore other shapes on the board or design boards with other shapes, e.g. triangular shapes, hexagons etc. It is possible to buy paper marked with these shapes. Of course this leads to exploration of tessellations of shapes.
3. They can move away from shapes to look at sequences of numbers themselves, e.g. odd numbers, multiples of 3 etc.

What the children can learn

Content
Number facts and skills. Relationships between numbers. Ideas about square numbers. Concepts of squaring numbers. Properties of shapes and tessellations.
Processes
Problem-solving approaches, starting with simple cases and then extending to more complex ones. Looking for patterns and relationships. Generalising and specialising. Drawing conclusions and justifying results.

Match Puzzle

Move the matches so that the bag of money is outside the container.

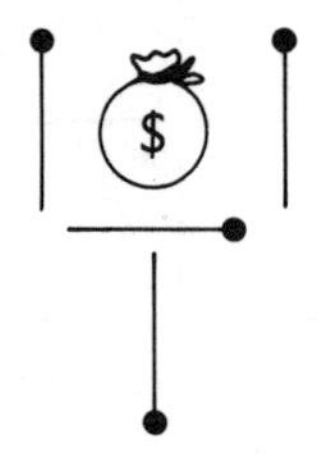

What is the least number of matches you need to move?

Comments

Ensure each child has the matches before commencing the puzzle. It is much easier to solve it this way, rather than using pencil and paper. Children will initially complete the puzzle in as many as eight moves and will need to be encouraged to solve it in less. Children could time themselves to see how quickly they can complete the task.

Extensions

1 This is strictly a puzzle but one that needs thought and can be extended, although the children do not always want to do that. It can be done moving only two matches, for example sliding the horizontal match to the right and moving the left-hand one to the right and below the horizontal match.
2 Encourage them to design their own puzzle.

What the children can learn

Content
The problem encourages the children to visualise the situation before they move the matches and therefore contributes to their understanding of spatial relationships.
Processes
Problem-solving by trial and reflection. Ability to explain ideas.

The Hundred Square

A hundred square looks like this.

1	2	3	4	5	6	7	8	9	10
11	12	13	14	15	16	17	18	19	20
21	22	23	24	25	26	27	28	29	30
31	32	33	34	35	36	37	38	39	40
41	42	43	44	45	46	47	48	49	50
51	52	53	54	55	56	57	58	59	60
61	62	63	64	65	66	67	68	69	70
71	72	73	74	75	76	77	78	79	80
81	82	83	84	85	86	87	88	89	90
91	92	93	94	95	96	97	98	99	100

A small square has been marked on the grid. It is a strange square with lots of number magic. What do you find when you add the four numbers in the corners of the square? Use a calculator if you wish.

1 + 3 + 21 + 23 =

The strange thing is that the number you get is related to **12**, the middle number in the square. Can you explain why this happens. What else can you find out?

Comments

There is a lot of arithmetic to do in this activity and a calculator is therefore a useful aid to avoid small errors. The children find that the total of the four corner numbers is 48, which is 4 times 12, the middle number. Encourage them to look at squares anywhere else on the grid. Also look for other relationships between numbers in the small square. There are a lot to find. The four middle numbers on the sides also total 4 times the one middle number. The pairs of opposite corner numbers give the same total as each other.

Extensions

1. Encourage the children to record their results.
2. Encourage them to explain, share and justify their results.
3. The small square can be changed into a 4 by 4 square. They can even try to have the square at an angle on the grid.
4. Try bigger or smaller squares or change the shapes. Try rectangles or triangles, or strange shapes like a letter 'T'.

What the children can learn

Content

Practice of number facts and skills. Recognising relationships between numbers that depend on addition or multiplication. Where appropriate, estimation skills and the use of a calculator.

Processes

Looking for patterns and relationships. Expressing these relationships using words, numbers or symbols. Generalising and specialising results. Predicting new patterns. Justifying relationships and patterns. Describing and explaining results.

Copying Each Other

Sit back-to-back with a partner. You each need a sheet of paper and a pencil. One of you draws a simple picture on your sheet and then tells the other how to draw it. Neither of you are allowed to look at the other's drawings. You are not allowed to use your hands to tell each other what to draw. When you have finished you can look at the two pictures. Take turns at giving the instructions. Try to work out how to help each other make the best copies.

Comments

This activity is a starting point for work on distance, direction and position, and links well with orienteering. It works well with any grade in primary schools. As it is very stimulating and lively it has to be done with the whole class. The children do need help in two aspects. Firstly they need to make the initial drawing simple, otherwise it can take too long and they become discouraged. Secondly they must avoid describing their drawings with words like 'draw a house with two windows'. To do so would prevent them learning to explain things with careful, precise and simple instructions. The intention is for them to learn how to specify a position on the page and how clear they need to be about distance and directions. Some children cannot move away from using words for whole objects and say 'draw a face, put in its eyes' etc. Others reach the point where they use instructions like 'pen down, draw a line 10 cm forward, turn right 90°'. These instructions are very close to the computer language *Logo* and we have used this activity very successfully as an introduction to *Logo*.

Extensions

1. The children enjoy the activity and would often ask to repeat it. We found it important to get them to talk about the types of instructions they used and how they could 'improve' on their copies.
2. A whole class version of this is to get the children to draw a picture on the blackboard while one member of the class is outside the room. The drawing is covered up and the child returns. Instructions are given to him/her to produce a copy of the original picture. This version allows the whole class to find new and better ways of giving instructions.
3. The robot version. One child acts the part of a robot (the turtle in *Logo*) and is blindfolded. The rest of the children direct him/her along a specified route or to a target. Reduce instructions to a minimum.
4. Introduce them to *Logo* and get them to explore ideas in it.
5. Groups prepare instructions for others to follow a course around the school or the local park, simulating orienteering.
6. Children are asked to describe their route from home to school and then sketch a map of it.

What the children can learn

Content

Distance and angles. Using centimetres. The concept of angles as an amount of turn. Half-turns, right angles and degrees. Estimation. Adding and subtracting amounts to reduce the number of commands. A right turn of 60 degrees followed by a left turn of 20 degrees is the same as a right turn of 40 degrees. How to undo unwanted movements—left 30 undoes right 30. Specifying position, the use of coordinates, bearings.

Processes

Describing and explaining. Listening and improving methods. Discussing and sharing. Generalising and convincing.

George compared people's weights at different times during the year. He used Sally's project from February to assist him with his exploration.

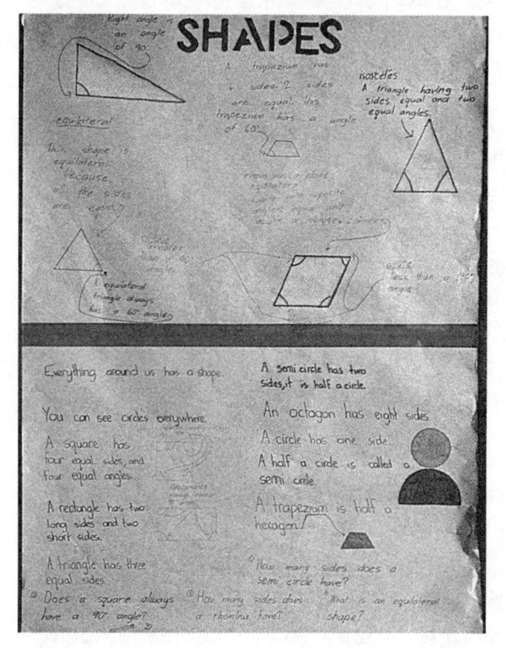

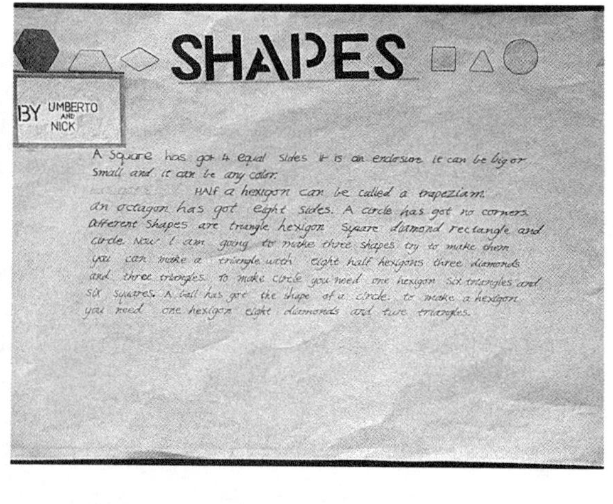

Two projects on shape showing the wide range in two children's understandings. This is a good example of how the program caters to the need of individuals, allowing each child to progress at their own rate.

Chapter Three

Creating an effective learning environment

Introduction

The quality of learning that occurs in any given classroom is a direct result of the type of learning environment that has been created by the teacher. Creating a positive and supportive environment is particularly important in maths because of the negative attitude that many children, parents and teachers have about the subject. Creating an effective learning environment involves:

- Immersing children in meaningful and purposeful explorations.
- Demonstrating ways of working with specific skills and problems, and positive attitudes about maths.
- Expecting children to: be able to solve problems, (girls especially need encouragement); share their struggles and achievements; support each others' learning; take responsibility for most of the decisions about their learning; be prepared to take 'risks' with their learning and make approximations in the process of developing strategies; and become actively engaged in solving problems of their own choice.

In establishing this kind of environment we are moving towards the creation of a community of learners in which children see themselves as researchers who are heavily reliant on both the environment and the people within it to support their learning.

In this chapter we will discuss ways in which teachers can support children's learning by developing a community of learners and creating a supportive physical environment.

Developing a community of learners

The major teaching/learning strategies used in developing a sense of community are:

- children taking responsibility
- children sharing
- modelling
- conferencing
- clinics

Children taking responsibility

1 Children taking responsibility for their own learning

When children take responsibility for their work, their level of commitment and enthusiasm for the task far exceeds anything we see when teachers make the decisions about what will be studied, when it will be studied, and how. Teachers who visited our classroom continually remarked on the enthusiasm that the children showed about their work—they were not only enthusiastic, but also very proud of the results of their research and experimentation.

In taking responsibility for their learning children must decide whether to work alone or in a small group. They will initially choose to work with friends (often resulting in groups based on ability). As they grow in confidence, encourage them to work in groups based on areas of interest rather than friendship. They must select a topic for exploration and decide on specific focus questions. Traditionally we have told children what they should learn and how they should learn it. When we now tell children that they can decide what they would like to learn about, this causes much insecurity, and most children do not know where to begin. This chapter discusses ways of assisting children in decision making. When children choose their own topics they do so in respect of their culture, gender, individual backgrounds and experiences. This means that the issues that they are exploring are very important on a personal level.

Children also need to decide a method for exploring their questions. Children are used to being told the appropriate ways to solve problems, but once they realise that teachers are serious about them exploring problems in their own ways, they will begin to experiment with different approaches. Two things that will assist children in this are ready access to a variety of resources, and the opportunity to share their ideas with their peers and teacher.

Children have to investigate the various ways of presenting their findings. They may initially present their findings in very elaborate ways and spend as much time on the presentation as they do on the exploration of their problems. As they gain confidence as researchers and experimenters, you will find that their commitment to finding out information will grow and they will choose ways of presenting their information that are appropriate but also quick and simple. Three of the more capable boys in our grade chose to keep a diary of their work and to make a summary of their findings at the end.

Children need to be able to acknowledge their own strengths and weaknesses in maths and seek assistance in developing new understandings through conferences with peers or teachers or attendance at Clinics (see page 77).

2 Children taking responsibility for the running of the classroom

> 'This room is great! I love it because we all get a say in how everything's run. If you've got a problem you just talk about it and you know everyone will help you solve it.'
>
> David, Grade 6

If we want children to be independent learners and thinkers who are able to make decisions that affect both themselves and others, then we need to share the running of the classroom with them.

Here are some suggestions on how to do this:

- Important issues arising in the classroom can be discussed, with the pros and cons of certain actions listed. Children then vote on the action they think to be the most appropriate. Discuss the importance of accepting and supporting the decision made, e.g. Should children be allowed to continue their maths projects for an extra week?
- Introduce private ballots for voting on major issues, e.g. Where do we want to go on our next excursion?
- When problems arise concerning behaviour, discuss them with the children to determine the appropriate means for solving the problem. Children are far more likely to accept the consequences for their behaviour if the decision is made by the whole class, not just the teacher.
- Children should be responsible for setting up class rules. These should be discussed and displayed by the children. Encourage children to write up rules in a positive rather than negative form. 'Don't run in the classroom' becomes 'Always walk in our room'.
- When having discussions children should be aware of the importance of giving everyone a fair go. It is often useful to suggest that the children put time limits on the speaker so that everyone has a say.

- If the teacher is to effectively model democracy in action, then sitting on the floor with the children during discussions is important—putting yourself in an elevated position only promotes the feeling that you are the superior member of the discussion and the main decision maker.
- Responsibilities and expectations of both the teacher and the children should be clearly defined. An excellent way of doing this is to record these on a large sheet of paper at the start of each day with the children's assistance. At the end of the day discuss these with the children to see if everyone was on target.

AREA	CHILDREN						TEACHERS					
MATHS PROJECT	• finish collecting data for projects • Conference with other children and teachers • Assist others in data collection • Begin publishing						• Assist children in collecting data • Give children ideas • Conference with all children • Provide at least 30 mins of Challenge Ladder					
	M	T	W	T	F	T	M	T	W	T	F	T
SCORE												
SCIENCE (WATER)	• write up at least two experiments with water • Test hypothesis • Assist children encountering problems with experimenting						• Provide support for all children • Organise one whole grade experiment including writing up the hypothesis • Conference where possible.					
	M	T	W	T	F	T	M	T	W	T	F	T
SCORE												

3 Contracts

Contracts are a means of giving responsibility to the learner by encouraging children to predict how long it will take them to complete and present research on a particular project. This encourages children to not only keep on target, but also to effectively plan their workloads. Contracts are also effective in assisting with classroom management.

Some suggestions for using contracts in the classroom:

- Explain to the children what a contract is and how it is used in society today.

CONTRACT

I Sally

PROMISE TO

have my information collected on how to make a bird cage.

BY May 25th 1988

SIGNED Sally

DATE May 18th 1988

- Brainstorm possible consequences for breaking a contract e.g. missing out on particular activities, extra duties etc.
- Give children the opportunity to extend existing contracts. Often children are unable to keep the contract due to over-committing themselves or interruptions to their normal routines.
- Not all children will need to work by contract. Introduce these on a needs basis. Often children will ask for a contract to keep themselves on target.

CONTRACT

I NICK

PROMISE TO

Behave a Lot better

BY 2 May

SIGNED NICK ✓

DATE 20\4\88

- Introduce whole class contracts to assist with classroom management.

CONTRACT

We Grade 5/6 S

PROMISE TO

help each other collect data

BY June 3rd

SIGNED Nicole – on behalf of grade 5 and 6.

DATE 28/5/88

- Sign a contract yourself in front of the class.

- Contracts should be displayed in a particular area of the classroom or kept by the teacher in the child's individual file.

Children sharing

Sharing is a powerful learning strategy that encourages children to develop a sense of themselves as a community of learners. When children share the difficulties they are encountering in their work, such as solving problems, locating resources or finding appropriate ways to present information, two things can happen:

i) they acknowledge, to themselves and others, that learning is often a struggle;

ii) an opportunity is created for another child to share their particular expertise or knowledge.

When children share their achievements they have an opportunity to show pride in their work.

1 Sharing at the whole class level

Incidental—the teacher interrupts the class to show or tell about a particular child's achievement. 'Jason's just found a new way to graph his results. What do you think about it?'.

At the end of a day's work—the teacher asks the children to share their struggles and/or achievements of the day.

e.g. 1: *Dimitra* 'I can't find any more information on parachutes.'
Angela 'My brother's got a book about the airforce. I'll ask him if I can bring it to school'.

e.g. 2: *Nicole* 'Do you want to know what a light year is?'

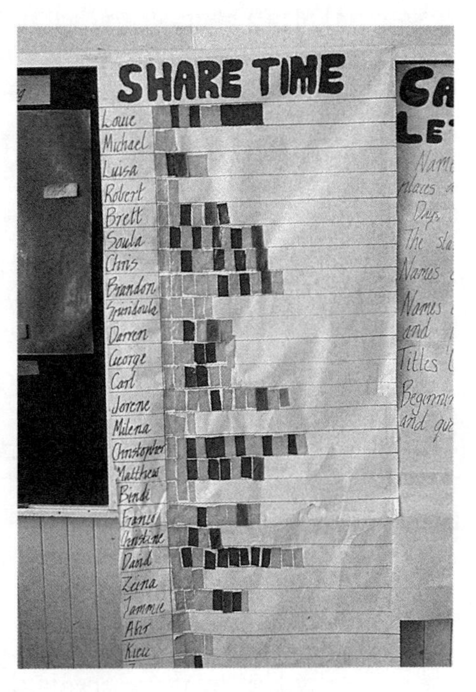

One way of sharing after the completion of projects. Children place a square next to their name after sharing their project with the grade.

On completion of a project—after the children have spent three weeks collecting data, conferencing with both peers and teacher, and finally publishing their work, they are very keen to get some public recognition for their work. Sharing their work with their peers provides an opportunity for both of the above mentioned things to happen.

2 Sharing on a one-to-one level

Getting ideas from each other—

e.g. *Umberto* 'I want to find out who has put on the most weight since February. Can I use the data on your maths project?'

Helping each other solve problems—children help each other with the skills they need to solve their problems as well as with difficulties associated with collecting, interpreting and presenting data.

e.g. *Maria* 'How do you know that the time in Italy is 7 hours earlier than in Melbourne?'

Alex 'Could you proofread my project please?'

Children should be encouraged to share their interests and feelings as well as their work. By providing the opportunity for children to share more personal aspects of themselves they are more likely to feel:

- accepted and supported by both their teachers and peers;
- positive about and aware of their strengths and weaknesses;
- confident to take risks in their learning.

Some suggestions on sharing

- Encourage children to write to each other on a regular basis. Brainstorm things to write about, e.g. likes, dislikes, personal problems, achievments, exciting events, invitations to each others homes, secrets, hobbies, etc.
- Keep a class diary where the events of each day or week are recorded. Children could fill this in on a rotational basis.
- Write to the children on an individual basis in a diary and encourage them to write back to you. This is an excellent way for children to communicate to you personal concerns as well as building up a good relationship with each child.
- Encourage children to arrange private conferences with you if they need to discuss problems or concerns.
- Give children a 'How I feel about' sheet at different stages throughout the year. Stress that these are confidential and encourage children to be honest when filling them out. After reading each sheet, call up each child for a private conference. During the conference discuss with the child ways of making negative feelings positive.

Name Michael Date

How do you feel about ?	
HAPPY O.K. SAD	
Reading	Sport
Writing	Lunch
Maths	Friends
Spelling	My Teacher
School	Playtimes
Home	Library
Art	Music

- Encourage children to be aware of each other's feelings and to comment on the positive attributes of class members. One way of doing this is to get children to write their name on the top of a blank sheet of paper. These sheets are then circulated around the room and each child writes one positive thing about each class member. When completed, each child can either read their own, or they can be shared as a whole grade.

Modelling

Both teachers and children are important role models within the learning process.

1 Teacher modelling

Teachers are significant adults within their students lives and as such have quite a powerful influence over the development of children's attitudes and skills. Teachers need to be aware of the power of modelling as a teaching strategy and to consciously plan to demonstrate:

- positive attitudes to maths;
- good work habits such as perseverance, motivation, independence and cooperation;
- the ability to use maths processes such as interpreting, recording and presenting data;
- the understanding that there are many different ways to solve a given problem;
- specific maths skills that will enable the children to be efficient and effective problem-solvers.

2 Child modelling

Children play a central role in each other's learning. They often learn by watching each other and copying. In a traditional classroom, copying is discouraged and not seen as contributing to children's learning. In this approach copying *is* encouraged. It allows children to observe how their peers solve mathematical problems, find relationships or present their findings.

Conferences

Conferences allow children to:

i clarify, confirm and extend their understandings;
ii seek support in their explorations.

Conferences allow teachers to:

i keep in touch with what all children are doing;
ii take an active interest in all children's work;
iii assist children with the selection, exploration, recording and sharing of their projects.

1 Teacher/student conferences

Conferences are an excellent means for the teacher to discuss with the children on an individual or small group basis their understandings of particular concepts and related skills. Conferences are also a time to assist children with the selection, exploration, recording and sharing of investigations/projects.

Here are some suggestions for setting up effective teacher/student conferences:

- Children should arrange conferences when needed by placing their names on a board for a particular day or session.
- Children who are waiting for a conference should be aware of activities they can do while waiting.
- Children should never disturb a conference unless it is an emergency.
- Encourage children to keep noise levels down during conferences. High noise levels can be very disruptive to the conference.
- Conferences should be brief, no longer than 5 to 10 minutes.
- Encourage children to come to the conference with a specific concern in mind, e.g. 'Can you show me how to find out how big our room is?'.
- During the conference, encourage children to identify what they need to do next and encourage them to concentrate on that point. Trying to deal with too many points only makes the child confused, overloaded and frustrated. It also lengthens the conference, giving you less time to conference with other children.
- At the conclusion of the conference, write down what the child or group is going to do next on a conference record sheet.
- Always respond to mathematical content before focusing on concerns about presentation or spelling and grammar.
- Never cross out or write on a child's draft. Encourage the children to record any necessary changes.
- During conferences, be positive and give encouragement.
- Encourage children to conference with each other before arranging a conference with you.
- Conduct roving conferences, moving around the room to assist children who need help, showing interest in their work and keeping an eye on their progress.

2 Student/student conferences

Children conferencing with each other has numerous advantages. Apart from encouraging the children to work cooperatively and supportively, it ensures that all children are given experiences in such processes as questioning, justifying, analysing, recommending, supporting, sharing and praising. Children conferencing with their peers encourages them to see each other as valuable resources and not to rely solely on you, the teacher. This strengthens their independence as learners, giving them greater responsibility for their own and other's learning.

Here are some suggestions for setting up effective peer conferences:

- Model and demonstrate effective ways to conference. Discuss with children questions that could be asked and responses that could be made. List these and encourage children to refer and add to the list when conferencing.
- Give children the opportunity to model a conference for the rest of the class. Discuss.
- Encourage children to look for the positive aspects of each other work first. Children should never criticise each others work, only make recommendations.
- Arrange a suitable area in the classroom where conferences can take place. This should be in a quiet area.
- Children should never disturb each other's conferences.
- Encourage children to organise their own system for arranging conferences.
- Sit in on children's conferences regularly and offer assistance. This is also a good way to monitor how children are coping with assisting each other in a conference situation.

Sample conference questions

Here are some conference questions you may find useful for teacher/student and peer conferences. These can be displayed to assist children when conferencing. Children should also be encouraged to come up with their own questions.

- Tell me about your investigation/project?
- What are you trying to find out?
- Who or what has helped you find this information?
- Is there anyone or anything that could give you more information?
- What are you going to do next?
- How are you going to present your findings? Some suggestions might be:
  - a book
  - a poster
  - a graph
  - a presentation
  - a video
  - a report
  - a demonstration.
- What new information have you found out since beginning your exploration?
  What type of maths have you used so far? e.g. addition, division, fractions, time, measurement, graphs, averages. How and why did you use this? Show me.
- Have you discussed your work with anyone else? If so, who? Did they give you any suggestions?
- Did you find out anything that surprised you?
- Have you used addition, subtraction, multiplication or division in your project? Can you show me where?

Ask questions that extend children's understandings and challenge them to explore further issues.

Clinics

Clinics are a teaching time specifically set aside to focus on a particular skill, with children taking responsibility for deciding whether or not they need to brush-up in this area. Clinics allow the teacher to give intensive instruction based on children's individual and group needs. As with writing clinics they should be based on the needs of the children and introduced as these needs become evident. Clinics can be introduced at any stage during the five week block and as regularly as needed. Below are some suggestions for setting up clinics within the maths program.

1 Attendance at clinics should be voluntary. Children need to be encouraged to identify their own needs and be responsible for attending clinics. The willingness to acknowledge their needs takes time to develop, but we found that in a supportive, non-threatening environment children did take on such responsibility. As the children became more confident with the approach and felt safe and secure within our classroom environment, we found that all those children who we had identified as needing to attend the clinic would attend. (Nelson would attend all clinics for a few minutes—once he realised that he

did understand the skill being discussed he would go on with his own work.)

2 A clinic noticeboard should be set up informing children when a clinic is to take place and what the subject matter will be. Children then place their name on the board to show that they wish to attend.

Initially some children may be hesitant to place their name on the board for fear of appearing inadequate or being ridiculed. But once a few names begin to appear, these children gradually overcome their fears and follow suit. It is good practice to place your name on the board demonstrating to the children that there is nothing wrong with wanting assistance in a particular area.

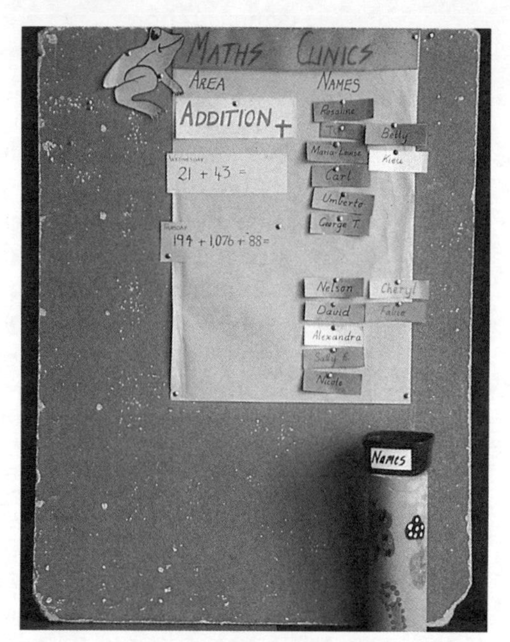

3 Discuss the role of clinics with the children and explain how they can help them in coming to terms with specific facts and skills that may be necessary in their projects. Ask children for suggestions about clinic topics and when and where they should be held in the classroom.

4 Specific skills being demonstrated should always relate back to concrete situations which the children understand. For example, if introducing a clinic on multiplication, discuss with the children when they need to use this skill in day-to-day life and in which projects they have explored multiplication skills. Introducing the skill in isolation only makes it appear irrelevant and useless.

5 Encourage children to look for different ways of working with the skill being discussed. If discussing subtraction, for example, get the children to find as many different ways they can of

finding the answer. Encourage children to share these different methods with each other. Remember there is not one method but many, and by discussing these you are giving the children a number of alternatives to choose from when solving their own problems in their daily life.

6 Children should be given specific tasks at the end of a clinic in order to consolidate and demonstrate their understandings, to themselves and the teacher, of the skill being discussed. This may be in the form of a group/individual activity or homework sheet of relevant problems. It is useful for the children to produce a chart or handout which can be referred to in times of uncertainty.

7 If some children have not understood the concept/skill being discussed, then try one or more of the following suggestions:
   - Hold another clinic on the same skill in a simpler form.
   - Encourage peer tutoring. Often children understand specific skills/concepts when they are explained to them by a peer.
   - Individually conference with the children to pinpoint where the lack of understanding is, then plan individual/group activities to help strengthen existing understandings.
   - Suggest a number of individual projects the children may like to explore which will strengthen existing understandings.

8 If the whole grade needs to attend a clinic, you could introduce it at the beginning or end of the maths session. If only one or two children need to attend a clinic, it is easier to call them up for a conference.

9 Always praise children who attend clinics. Some children may have a good understanding of the skill being discussed but wish to attend the first part of the clinic to confirm their understandings—praise these children also.

10 Always inform children who are not attending a clinic to work quietly on their projects and not to interrupt the clinic.

11 Keep a record of children attending each clinic and note to what extent the skill was understood by the children attending. See Chapter 4 for more detail.

12 Keep clinics short and to the point, children will be anxious to continue their own projects and will be reluctant to attend a clinic if they feel that it will take too much of their time—15 minutes is the maximum you should allow.

Establishing a community of learners can also be facilitated by:

- Setting up a classroom fund so children can purchase items for the classroom when going on holidays or to special events.
- Having a class mascot. Last year our class had Chadwick P. Bear, complete with clothes and personal belongings. Chadwick's experiences included being read to, being the focus of stories and projects, being taken home by children on a roster system and even being on the class roll. Chadwick belonged to the grade and he provided the children with a personal focus. We often saw the children teaching Chadwick concepts introduced to them earlier, showing us their level of understanding.
- Playing games that involved the whole grade. A game that we played frequently was Pulse. This involves the children sitting in a circle on the floor and joining hands. The leader begins by squeezing the hand of the person next to them. That person in turn squeezes the hand of the person next to them and on it goes until the pulse gets back to the leader. A timer is appointed and children see how quickly the pulse takes to go around the circle. Our record time for 28 children was .65 of a second. Can you beat that?

Creating a supportive physical environment

Creating a supportive physical environment involves:
- Setting up a maths area.
- Organising displays.
- Caring for the environment.

Setting up a maths area

The maths area should contain a range of resources to support children's explorations, games and problems that can be used to stimulate the children's curiosity and excitement, and a display of children's completed projects that can be used as reference points for other explorations.

A class project could be to set up the area by bringing in the following items for loan to the classroom. You could advertise in the school's newsletter for particular items. Opportunity Shops are also a great resource.

matches plastic cups counting frames
containers of sand, rice, macaroni, tea, oats, beans, etc
empty containers in various shapes and sizes
metre rulers measuring tapes clocks
buckets weights compasses
string wool
blocks lego cardboard
paper (various sizes) scissors
beads M.A.B. blocks jugs
cardboard boxes stop watches height chart
measuring spoons tapes (sticky and masking)
drawing pins Textas crayons
pens and pencils play money paint
puzzles and brain teasers elastic bands
shopping catalogues erasers
information booklets on time, money, space, etc
playing cards
commercially produced games play-doh
ice-cream sticks ruled-up grid bottle tops
computer and software

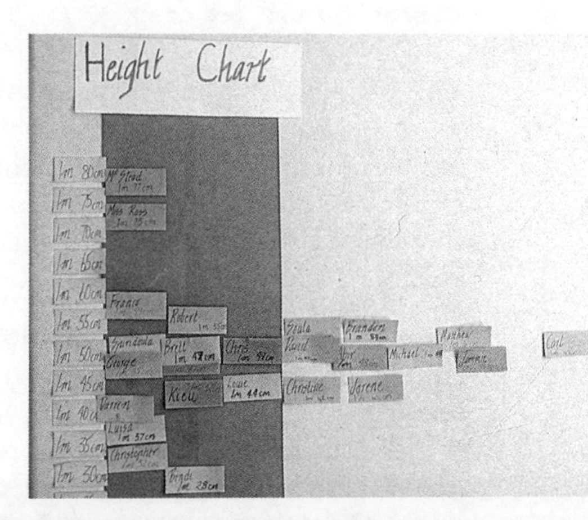

Organising displays

Teacher displays

Teacher displays provide children with reference points that they can use in times of uncertainty. For example, if the concept of addition had been discussed in a clinic, it would be useful to make a small display so that children and teachers could refer to this when needed.

This allows the children to become more independent in their learning by encouraging them to look to the environment for information required rather than relying solely on the teacher.

Here are some ideas for teacher displays:

1 Allow children to assist in creating the display. This will help to consolidate the information discussed.
2 Displays should be centred around class/group discussions. Constructing a display before the concept has been discussed does not give the children an active say and assumes that you have all the information and the children have nothing to contribute.
3 If a child is encountering difficulties, encourage him/her to refer to displays before coming to you for the information.
4 Refer to existing displays on a regular basis so that children are always aware of where particular information is should they need it.
5 Model, demonstrate and discuss different ways of displaying information.
6 Encourage children to add newly found information to existing displays.

Children's displays

> 'It's great having our work up because it makes our room look pretty and it makes me happy to see color everywhere. It's also great because people can get ideas from each other. I like this room better than my bedroom.'
>
> Sally, Grade 5

Children, like all of us, are proud of what they produce. Nothing is more rewarding than seeing work we have taken time and effort to produce, displayed for all to admire and learn from. It is this recognition that motivates children to not only produce more, but to make each production better than the last.

Apart from making the environment colorful and pleasing to the eye, displays enhance our self-confidence, reward us for the efforts we have made and are a ready source of information for others.

When children take an active role with displays they are taking responsibility for their environment as well as supporting other children's learning, both of which help in creating a community of learners.

Here are some ideas for displaying children's work:

Do

1 Let the children decide where to display their work. Giving them an active say in the display of work will ensure care for and love of their environment.
2 Change displays on a regular basis after consultation with the children. Old displays are not a true indication of the work

children are currently producing and tend to make the environment stale.

3 Let children help in the putting up and taking down of displays. It gives them responsibility in creating and changing the environment. It also fosters in them care for other children's work as well as developing in them aesthetic awareness.
4 Refer to work after it has been displayed. Congratulate children on their efforts and encourage them to praise each other.
5 Encourage other children, teachers, parents and ancillary staff to come into the classroom to look at the children's work. This will help build up the children's self-confidence.
6 Encourage children to take their work home either before or after it has been displayed. Suggest to children that they display work at home and show their friends and family.

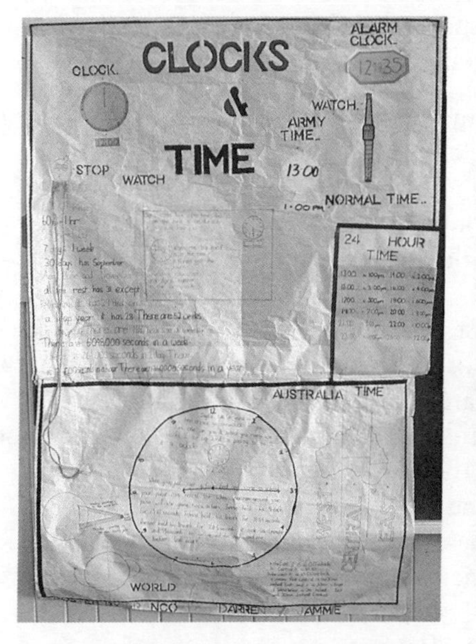

Don't

1 Display work unless you have first asked the children if they want their work on display. If children are not completely satisfied with their work, displaying it will only make them feel embarrassed and inadequate—give them the responsibility for making the decision.
2 Take down displays if they are still being used or admired. Consult with children first and encourage them to discuss the worth of retaining particular displays.
3 Throw away old displays. Encourage children to file past works in a large folder and compare these with current endeavours. This serves as an excellent means for children to evaluate their individual progress throughout the year.
4 Put up displays where they cannot be adequately viewed.

Caring for the environment

'Having a nice room with lots of our work up makes me happy and makes me want to come to school because it looks great and makes me proud of what we do. When you're in here you want to stay because it's so comfortable. If we had to work from the blackboard or worksheets it would be so boring. I wouldn't learn anything, I'd just daydream.'

Nicole, Grade 5

If children are encouraged to bring objects from home and time is spent on both displays and setting up a maths area, then children need to feel that the environment will remain cared for and that the risk of damage will be minimal. It is best if all children take on a feeling of responsibility for the environment, rather than just a few children who have been allocated as monitors. It is also important for the teacher to be aware that the learning environment can be greatly affected by natural conditions such as airflow, heat, cold and light. Uncomfortable natural conditions make learning difficult, despite aesthetically pleasing surroundings.

Here are some suggestions:

1. Help in the cleaning, don't leave it all to the children. By assisting, you are modelling and demonstrating that you too care for the environment.
2. Praise the children in their efforts in keeping the environment tidy.
3. Don't criticise the untidiness of children's lockers or desks if your desk is also untidy. Remember, practise what you preach.
4. Allow adequate time each day for cleaning up.
5. Ensure all children know where equipment and resources belong.
6. Discuss with the children the importance of keeping the environment clean and tidy.
7. Make sure there are adequate cleaning tools.
8. Furnishing the room with objects from the children's homes, such as:

plants/flowers	soft toys
cushions/beanbags	birthday cards
books/magazines	ornaments
clothes to dress up in	games
photos	personal drinking mugs

Chapter Four

Evaluation and record keeping

The intention of this program is to promote children's learning of mathematics in our classrooms. To ensure this happens the program needs a method of evaluation and record keeping that fits in with the natural conditions of learning as discussed in Chapter 1. Children need feedback on the work they are engaged in. This feedback needs to acknowledge the quality of their endeavours and the value of their ideas. The feedback also needs to show them the progress they are making in the acquisition of mathematical facts, skills, understanding and processes and in the development of their personal qualities. The feedback needs to be given from a wide variety of sources and contexts.

Traditional approaches use evaluation to decide what the needs of the children are and what content needs to be provided for each child. The children are then 'plugged' into appropriate textbooks or activities. This evaluation depends on the teacher alone, is often seen as an activity separate from normal teaching and is often structured in a formal manner.

In contrast, the approach in this program does not depend on placing children at the right point of a pre-written textbook. In all parts of the program children are expected to take responsibility for their own learning. They choose activities that they are interested in or are important for them. They therefore work on these at their own levels and they ask the teacher for the help they need. Establishing the exact level for each of the children is therefore not as vital. It is more important for the children to get feedback on their work from the teacher and the other children. Nevertheless it is accepted that careful evaluation of children's learning is needed. The teachers need to be able to inform parents and future class teachers about the children. They also require information on what the children can do within the program. For example, teachers need to know which children should be encouraged to take further risks with their learning. They can suggest that children vary the activities they choose or try more difficult ideas or approaches.

Evaluation in this program is seen in the wider sense of collecting information on the children from a wide variety of sources and then using it when giving them advice or help or when passing information about the children to others. In describing the evaluation process we discuss below the following aspects:

- Guidelines for evaluation.
- What is evaluated.
- When evaluation occurs.
- How evaluation is carried out.
- Methods of record keeping.

Guidelines for evaluation

In setting up the evaluation for the program the following guidelines were used:

1 The evaluation processes must be an integral part of the program, continually providing feedback to the child, the teacher, and parents. It is therefore part of normal class activities.

2 The evaluation procedures must fit in with our beliefs on how children learn. The importance of giving responsibility to children is to have them become active participants in their own evaluation and in feedback to each other.

3 Evaluation is only done when it is useful, either feeding into teaching or leading to some specific action.

4 It is acknowledged that aspects within evaluation in any program are subjective. This brings with it problems related to the backgrounds of the children, including issues to do with gender, ethnicity, class or language. This program, with its stress on placing learning within contexts the child determines, addresses these issues through raising teachers' awareness of the children as individuals.

5 Evaluation must be constructive. It focuses on what the children can do, and not what they cannot do. It looks for the child's strengths and through that encourages further learning by creating a positive atmosphere and positive self-images.

6 The involvement of the children in their own evaluation increases their motivation.

7 Evaluation must not be a destructive burden to the teacher. It occurs when facts, skills and concepts, processes and personal qualities are observed in individual children.

What is evaluated?

As was discussed in Chapter 1, this maths program is aimed at children's knowledge and understanding of concepts in mathematics and the associated facts and skills, developing and using a range of mathematical processes, and developing personal qualities.

Body of knowledge

The range of mathematical knowledge is subdivided into the following categories:

- *Number*—counting, number names, place value, pattern and order, negative numbers
- *Whole numbers*—four operations
- *Decimals*—place value, order, operations
- *Fractions*—notation, simple ordering
- *Percentages*
- *Measurement*—length, area, volume and capacity, mass, time, money
- *Visual representation*—representing data in various forms, e.g. tables, diagrams, pictures, graphs
- *Spatial relations*—two and three dimensional shapes and their properties, position, angles, symmetry and movement.

Processes

The mathematical processes that the children meet, learn about and use are listed below. They are grouped in similar types to make them easier to use. The list is intended as a 'pool' of processes for teachers to base their thoughts on as they evaluate the progress the children are making in their use of mathematical processes. The list is not complete and teachers would need to extend the list as their experience with their children in the program grows.

identifying, classifying, sorting
ordering
estimating and approximating
questioning, challenging, hypothesising
experimenting and testing
monitoring and collecting data
recording and processing data
relating and looking for relationships
specialising and generalising
reasoning, justifying
describing, explaining
communicating, presenting

Personal qualities

The personal qualities that can be developed during the program are listed below. These qualities develop over the whole curriculum for each child. The ones listed are those most desired in mathematics sessions. The list is not complete but is intended to provide class teachers with a 'thesaurus' of ideas to help them assess the children's development.

independence
cooperation

responsibility
attitude
patience
care, acceptance
consideration
flexibility
motivation
appreciation
confidence
supportive, pride in their work
willingness to share
perseverence

When evaluation occurs in the program

Evaluation occurs:
- during and after whole group explorations;
- in clinics;
- during whole grade discussions;
- in sharing sessions;
- when the children are filling in their project plans;
- during individual conferences;
- during small group conferences;
- while the children are working on their projects;
- after completion of their projects;
- during and after work on investigations and puzzles;
- when the children are involved in self-evaluation tasks;
- informally when children are explaining, justifying, debating, and questioning ideas and concepts.

How evaluation is carried out

The teacher carries out evaluation by:
- arranging regular conferences with each child;
- listening to what a child is saying whenever possible;
- observing the feedback a child gives other children on their work;
- observing the ways a child tackles problems, the processes used and the personal qualities shown;
- observing the way a child interacts with others;
- monitoring a child's attendance at clinic sessions;
- monitoring conferences held with a child and what is discussed at each;
- monitoring share-time sessions and comment sheets;
- monitoring a child's self-assessment tasks.

Record keeping—What do I keep where?

The description below is a full record-keeping structure used in the program. It is not intended to be prescriptive and it is expected that teachers will either implement it gradually or modify it to suit their own ideas.

Records are kept in three places: the teacher's Work Program; the child's Personal Folder; and the Individual Files. Each of these, together with details of the items in them, are described below. In each case an actual example of the records on a child is included.

The teacher's work program

The teacher's work program holds:

- conference record sheets
- clinic records

Conference record sheets

These give the teacher an overall picture of which children have been attending conferences at regular intervals. Teachers need to fill this in after each conference by placing the date the conference was held next to the child's name. Teachers should check this sheet at least once a week to ensure all children are attending conferences on a regular basis. (Refer to charts at end of chapter.)

Clinic records

These records provide the teacher with information on the clinics the child has attended and the specific facts, skills and concepts the child understands. This information needs to be transferred to the child's profile. (Refer to charts at end of chapter.)

The child's personal folder

The personal folders hold:

- project plans
- projects
- sharetime comments

Project plans

These allow the teacher to monitor the children's progress in planning an investigation. By constantly reviewing these plans the teacher is able to see the types of investigations the child is involved in and how the child goes about exploring. Project plans need to be collected by the teacher at regular intervals and current plans compared with earlier efforts to monitor progress made by the child. Relevant information can then be extracted and recorded on the child's profile. (Refer to charts at end of chapter.)

Projects

After projects have been completed the teacher needs to collect these to determine what mathematical facts, skills and concepts were explored by the child. This, together with observations of the child in action, assist the teacher in filling out the child's profile. Copies of the child's project in either draft or published form are kept by the child in their personal file or may be on display. The teacher needs to compare existing projects with earlier ones to monitor the child's progress.

Share-time comments

Comments made by the child during sharing sessions give the teacher information on the child's ability to:

- share and reflect upon the project they have just completed;
- share and reflect upon other children's projects;
- ask relevant questions to extract information;
- identify important issues that need to be considered in future projects.

Written share-time comments are kept by the child but should be used by the teacher to assist in filling out student profiles. (Refer to charts at end of chapter.)

The Individual Files

The Individual Files (kept by teacher but available to the child) hold;

- conference discussion sheets
- self-evaluation tasks
- student profile sheets

Conference discussion sheets

These are a clear record of the issues discussed with the child during conferences and what action the child decided to take after the conference. This allows the teacher to have a clear picture of exactly what task each child is involved in and who they are working with. Conference discussion sheets are filled in by the teacher after each conference and are constantly reviewed to extract information to record on the child's profile sheets. They are kept by the teacher in the child's individual file but need to be made available to the child should they need to re-check the task set. (Refer to charts at end of chapter.)

Self-assessment tasks

Frequently throughout the year the teacher needs to design self-evaluation tasks to monitor each child's attitude towards their learning. These tasks give a picture of how the children view their own mathematical development, their attitudes and feelings towards mathematics and their view of the program. These may take the form of questionaires, surveys, reports, diaries or interviews. Relevant information from these tasks are used to fill in the children's profile sheets. (Refer to charts at end of chapter.)

Student profile sheets

The profile serves as means of combining all the data on each child collected by the teacher. This gives the teacher an overall picture of each child's development in mathematical concepts, skills and facts as well as the personal qualities the child displays and the processes used. The profile also serves as a means of monitoring action that needs to be taken to further develop and support each child's learning. Data used to fill out the profile is collected from the child's personal folder, individual file, records kept by the teacher in their work program, as well as constant observations of the child in action and the work they produce. The profile is a valuable source of information to assist the teacher in compiling reports for parents and the child's future teachers. The teacher needs to fill in each child's profile on a regular basis to ensure constant monitoring of their learning. (Refer to charts at end of chapter.)

Conference Record Sheet

Name	Dates of Conferences Attended																
ROSALINE	18/2	21/2	12/3	1/4	3/4	8/4	5/5	6/5	7/5	9/6	21/6	17/7	21/7	6/8	20/8	10/10	1/11	1/12
CARL	20/2	22/2	10/3	2/4	3/4	5/4	12/4	4/5	3/6	10/6	28/6	18/7	27/7	6/8	19/8	2/10	2/11	20/11
DAVID	19/2	21/2	8/3	4/4	5/4	6/5	4/6	27/6	19/7	20/7	18/8	2/10	5/11	20/11	2/12			
MARIA-LOUISE	17/2	20/2	7/3	8/3	1/4	2/4	1/5	3/5	6/5	7/5	9/6	20/6	17/7	18/7	21/7	5/8	20/8	21/8
TIM	17/2	7/3	9/3	3/4	8/4	4/5	6/5	10/6	21/6	17/7	18/7	19/7	20/7	1/8	6/8	30/9	5/11	20/11
ALEX	18/2	6/3	7/3	8/4	4/5	5/5	10/6	17/7	1/8	2/8	30/9	5/11	1/12	10/12				
KIEU	18/2	19/2	13/3	1/4	3/4	8/4	6/5	7/5	9/5	9/6	21/6	18/7	21/7	7/8	20/8	11/10	11/11	
GEORGE	18/2	7/3	9/3	4/4	7/4	3/5	7/5	8/5	9/6	10/6	20/6	21/6	18/7	21/7	6/8	6/9	1/10	10/10
VOULA	21/2	6/3	9/3	4/5	6/5	10/6	11/6	21/6	18/7	19/8	20/8	30/9	5/11	2/12	3/12			
SALLY R.	19/2	5/3	6/3	8/4	4/5	5/5	27/5	28/6	18/7	19/7	6/8	19/8	2/9	10/10	11/10	1/12		
JASON	23/2	24/2	8/3	4/4	6/4	6/5	7/5	9/5	20/6	21/6	18/7	20/7	6/8	20/8	29/9	14/10	1/11	2/11
FABIO	20/2	7/3	9/3	17/3	24/4	1/5	7/5	3/6	9/6	21/6	18/7	27/7	19/8	1/9	2/9	2/10	3/10	4/10

Conference Record Sheet

Name	Dates of Conferences Attended																	
SALLY E	20/2	6/3	9/3	4/5	27/6	17/7	5/8	21/8	29/9	11/11	2/12							
PETER	21/2	22/2	5/3	5/5	20/6	17/7	21/8	29/9	3/11	2/12	10/12	11/12						
NICOLE	20/2	5/3	17/3	4/4	27/5	21/6	18/7	6/8	30/9	3/11	11/11	1/12	5/12	7/12				
UMBERTO	17/2	8/3	8/4	3/5	8/5	10/6	18/7	19/7	6/8	19/8	29/9	2/10	10/11	11/11	12/11	2/12	3/12	
TONIA	24/2	9/3	8/4	3/5	9/5	17/6	18/6	13/7	8/8	19/8	25/9	5/10	10/11	2/12	4/12	5/12		
APHRODITE	24/2	2/4	3/5	9/5	10/6	17/7	23/7	19/8	30/9	3/10	14/11	15/11	1/12	2/12				
NICK	23/2	9/3	8/4	3/5	8/5	11/6	19/7	20/7	19/8	1/9	2/9	6/9	2/10	1/11	5/12			
DIMITRA	22/2	27/2	9/3	9/4	8/5	9/5	11/6	20/7	19/8	1/9	2/9	6/9	29/9	1/10	2/10	11/11	4/12	5/12
NELSON	20/2	9/3	2/4	8/4	3/5	8/5	9/6	10/6	19/7	6/8	19/8	30/10	2/12					
BETTY	19/2	20/2	5/3	9/3	24/3	24/4	25/4	7/5	20/5	20/6	28/7	29/7	6/8	29/8	14/10	1/11	2/11	1/12
DAMIEN	19/2	8/3	5/5	22/6	16/7	17/7	30/9	1/11	1/12									

Record of a clinic (from work program)

Front View

> WEDNESDAY OCTOBER 10TH
>
> Addition E.g. 24 + 179 + 97 =

Displayed on clinic board for children to see

Back View

> CHILDREN ATTENDED/COMMENTS
>
> √ Marisa – Completed a homework task – understands how to tackle this.
>
> Rosaline – Still encountering difficulties – will need further work in this area.
>
> √ Jason – Stayed at Clinic for first 5 minutes to confirm understandings.
>
> √ Michael – Completed homework task – understandings clear.
>
> Peter – Still having problems – further work needed.

After clinic comments are made and this is placed in the teacher's work program

Project Plan

Names Nelson, Nicole, Tonia

Date 11/10

Topic Planets

What we know

See attached

What we don't know

Other solar systems
Size of all planets
Temperature of all the planets
How far the planets are from the sun
How much air we need to live
Moons on other planets

What we want to find out

How far the planets are from the sun, what moons they have, their temperature, their orbits, their size. How fast a rocket goes.

How we will use maths in the program

length, adding up distances, finding out about temperatures, speeds.

How we will find out our information

From books, other people, our parents, the library, experimenting.

Approved Cheryl 12/10

What we know

what about other solar systems?

There are nine planets in our solar system

They are the Earth, Saturn, Venus, Pluto,

Mars, Jupiter, Mercury, Uranis and Neptune.

what size are all the planets?

saturn is the biggest planet Mercury is

the hottest planet because its closest to

how hot? How far away are the other planets?

the sun. The earth takes a year to

go around the sun and a day to spin

Explain.

around. You get to the moon in a

rocket and it takes about three

how fast does it go?

months. We cant live on any other

planet because there is not enough

How much air do we need?

air there for us to breathe. Some

other planets have moons like us.

how many moons?

what size are they?

Sharetime Comments

1. What improvements have you noticed?

More colour. Lots of information that you can understand. Good headings. Good pictures. I really like the way Sally R. presented her information. Some of the ideas were fantastic. Carl had lots of good information much more than last time. Things were set out much better.

2. How can the projects be improved next time?

Too many spelling mistakes and some of them need to be neater. Some didn't give you enough information. Our handwriting is getting better but we still need more practise. Some people don't explain things enough and they don't all make sense.

3. Which projects did you like the most and why?

Peter and Fabios one was very interesting because it had the longest and shortest things in the world. It was sort of like the Guiness book of records but easier to read. Tania and Aphios had lots of information I didn't know about it was really good.

4. What ideas did you get for your next project?

Lots. I want to do one like Peter and Fabios only I'm going to do the heaviest things in the world.

5. What things about maths did you learn from the projects?

I learnt what the longest things and the shortest things are. I found out how to weigh my hand and who has the heaviest hand in the grade. I didn't know what volume meant but now I do and I think I learnt that maths is not just sums but lots of things.

Conference Discussion Sheet Name Carl

Date	Discussion Points/Action
20/2	Carl and I talked about his project plan on the perimeter of the school. Carl will give me more information on how he is going to do this.
22/2	Information given. Carl will begin project.
10/3	Carl and I discussed the best way to publish the information he has gathered. We decided on a report.
2/4	Talked about topic for next project, Carl will talk to David and Voula to get more ideas.
3/4	Topic decided. Carl will begin project plan.
6/4	Plan approved. Investigation will begin.
12/4	Carl is having problems specialising in his project - he is clear now, after our talk. Will work with David on a combined project.
4/5	Doesn't want to share with whole grade - we discussed this issue, Carl and David will share with a small group.
3/6	Discussed concept of capacity arising from whole grade project - Carl will do a project with Sally R to extend understandings.

Conference Discussion Sheet

Name: Carl

Date	Discussion Points/Action
10/6	Approval given for project plan.
28/6	Discussed project and what Carl and Sally learnt from the project.
18/7	Carl is concerned about using multiplication (skills). Suggested he attend next clinic group.
27/7	Project plan discussed - asked Carl to justify the mathematical content.
6/8	Discussed methods of gathering information with Carl, Tim and David (Space project).
19/8	Project discussed. Talked about self assessment task (Tim will help Carl overcome concerns).
2/10	Carl wants to produce a booklet of games for part three of the program, approval given.
2/11	Called Carl for a conference to discuss his work.
20/11	Orienteering course with Alex – successful.

Self Assessment Task

Date 19th August

Name Jason

1. Do you like maths? Why/Why not?

I love maths this year because we get to do projects about things we like. I reckon I learn more when I do projects. I use to hate maths because it was boring.

2. What are you good at in maths?

I'm good at solving problems and finding out things. I know heaps about money and time.

3. What do you need more help in?

I think I need to go to a clinic on ÷ because sometimes I get confused but not all the time.

4. Do you like the new way we do maths?

Yes it's heaps better than the old way. You don't learn much when you have to do sums on the black board. In the new way I like it when you can work with other kids. The share times are good because you learn things you didn't know about and it gives you ideas.

5. What ways can we improve this?

More time for projects. We need more Maths time.

Self Assessment Task

Interviews 27/2/88	Interviews
TEACHER: "What is maths?" ALEX: "Lots of things, sums, x tables, divisions and things like that."	TEACHER: "What is maths?" ALEX: "The time, volume, area; it's about learning and finding out things. It's working out solutions. You can use maths everywhere you go, for example, when you pull a chair out of a table you need to know how far to pull it out so you can fit in – this is maths."
TEACHER: "What is maths?" GEORGE: "Adding up, weight, volume and lots of sums."	TEACHER: "What is maths?" GEORGE: "Maths is time, it's if you go to the shop, knowing how much change to get so you don't get ripped off. Maths is being able to read the time, it's the seasons, the days, the months. It's knowing when it's your birthday. It helps you through your life. Maths is how long it takes the sun to go around the earth, it's being able to use a calculator, a computer. Maths is everything.
TEACHER: "What is maths?" VOULA: "It's sums to do with numbers."	TEACHER: "What is maths?" VOULA: "Maths is using things. Maths is shopping and working out how much things are and if you have enough to pay for them. It's nearly everything, you use it at school, at home, everywhere.

Student Profile

Page One

Name ALEX Grade 5 Year 1988

BODY OF KNOWLEDGE	CONCEPT	FACT/SKILL	COMMENTS AND ACTION
NUMBER counting place value order	(2/5) Place value understood (20/6) Sees patterns in number	Can count by 2's → 12's (10/3) Can order numbers knows > < (20/6) Can read, write and order numbers	(15/3) Introduced rounding off to nearest 10, 100, as part of project (successfully used).
+	(20/4) Understands when to use addition in solving problems.	(20/4) 2 and 3 digit no's (10/10) 4 and 5 digit no's	(10/10) Able to use calculator to check algorithms.
−	(21/4) Knows when to use subtraction in day to day life	(21/4) 2 digit (mentally) 3 digit algorithms (11/11) 4 digit algorithms	(11/11) Calculator used successfully to check algorithms
×	(1/12) Understands effect of multiplying by 10, 100, 1000	(1/5) Tables up to 12 (mentally) 2 digit x 1 digit algorithms (11/11) 2 digit x 2 digit algorithms	(1/5) Can use calculator
÷	(2/10) Can relate to day to day life	(2/10) 2 digit by 1 digit algorithm	(2/10) Calculator used successfully.

BODY OF KNOWLEDGE	CONCEPT	FACT/SKILL	COMMENTS AND ACTION
DECIMALS place value order operations	(20/9) Understands decimals in terms of money (11/11) Understands decimals in terms of length, mass and time.	(20/9) Use decimal notation as a way of recording money (11/11) Decimal notation to 2 places in context of measurement	(20/9) Extend knowledge into other measurement areas (11/11) Successfully extended ✓
FRACTIONS	(20/9) Understands fractions in day to day life	(20/9) Can estimate fraction of a whole - ½ ⅓ ¼	
PERCENTAGE	(4/5) Demonstrates little understanding of concept (11/11) Understands percentage as a fraction of something	(11/11) Can calculate percentage of something out of 100.	(4/5) Introduce as part of whole grade exploration

Student Profile **Page Two**

Name ALEX Grade 5 Year 1988

BODY OF KNOWLEDGE	CONCEPT	FACT/SKILL	COMMENTS AND ACTION
LENGTH	(5/3) Good understanding of relationships between units	(5/3) Can use formal units - cm, metre, kilometre, millimetre (1/7) Able to estimate	(5/3) No further action needed at this stage.
AREA	(5/3) Good understanding of estimation (10/10) Understands formula	(5/3) Able to find area of a four sided shape - unfamiliar with specific formula (10/10) Can use formula L x W	(5/3) Introduce specific formula later on in the year if she doesn't self discover it. (8/10) Specific formula introduced.
VOLUME CAPACITY	(20/4) Understandings unclear (3/6) Understandings much clearer (10/10) Understands displacement	(20/4) Can estimate using pints not litres (3/6) Can use formal units of litres, millilitres	(20/4) Suggest Alex works with other children to extend existing knowledge (3/6) Alex explained her understandings to Carl during a share session (understandings confirmed).
MASS	(1/5) Excellent understandings Able to see its importance in day to day life	(1/5) Good vocabulary Can use grams, kg (1/7) Able to estimate	(1/5) No further action needed at this stage

BODY OF KNOWLEDGE	CONCEPT	FACT/SKILL	COMMENTS AND ACTION
TIME	20/8 Concept good, knows relationships between different units	20/8 Can use sec, minutes, hrs, knows about 24 hr clock. Can tell time, estimate and work out problems 11/11 Can use a timetable	20/8 Suggested Alex work with Rosaline to share her knowledge.
MONEY	11/10 Excellent understandings of both our currency and Greek currency. Can apply knowledge.	11/10 Confident in using all units	11/10 No further action needed.
VISUAL REPRESENTATION	21/4 Understands bar graph information. 11/10 Understands line graph.	21/4 Can produce bar graph to represent data 11/10 Can produce line graph to show data	21/4 Introduce other forms of representation in whole grade focus.
SPATIAL RELATIONS	10/5 Good understandings of shapes in the environment 1/7 Relationship between shapes becoming evident 20/8 Clear understandings of 2 & 3 dimensional	10/5 Knows about squares, rectangles, circles, diamonds 1/7 Knows about rhombuses, octagons, pentagons. 20/8 Able to complete orienteering course.	10/5 Extend existing understandings through next whole grade focus 20/8 Understandings extended.

Student Profile

Page Three

Name *Alex* Grade *5* Year *1988*

PROCESSES	PERSONAL QUALITIES
Identifying, classifying, sorting, ordering, estimating, questioning, challenging, hypothesising, experimenting, testing, monitoring, collecting data, recording, processing, representing, interpreting, relating, specialising, generalising, justifying, explaining, describing, communicating, presenting.	*Independence, co-operation, responsibility, attitude, patience, care, perserverance, acceptance, consideration, flexibility, motivation, appreciation, confidence, supportive, pride, sharing.*
OBSERVATIONS/ACTIONS	**OBSERVATIONS/ACTIONS**
(20/2) Able to identify, classify and sort. (5/3) More experiences needed in estimating. (15/3) Project showed Alex is able to collect a wide variety of data, able to sort, process and interpret data. (3/4) Needs to develop questioning techniques (conferenced over this issue). (20/4) Able to justify (orally) – Can convince other children. (4/5) Questioning techniques are developing. (10/5) Project demonstrated Alex is developing a wide range of processes, she is far more confident in testing, monitoring and hypothesing. (3/6) Excellent communication skills. (1/7) Estimating skills improving – suggest that future projects involve this process. (5/8) Finds specialising difficult – Arrange conference. (20/8) Project work indicates a strong development in all processes. (10/10) Specialising skills evident. (1/12) Satisfied with Alex's development in using mathematical processes.	(20/2) Very co-operative, has a positive attitude towards learning. (10/3) More patience and perserverance needed – discussion point for next conference. (3/4) Loves sharing, gives support to other class members. (1/5) Confidence growing. (10/5) Greater patience and perserverance noted on last project. (1/7) Extremely responsible and supportive of other class members. (20/8) Motivation lagging – may need different direction – discuss with her. (22/8) Back on task. (1/12) Displays a wide range of personal qualities. Is seen by the class as a strong role model and a terrific helper.

Bibliography

AINLEY J and BOLDSTEIN R *Making Logo Work—A guide for teachers* Blackwell 1988

ALLEN P *Who sank the boat?* Nelson, Melbourne, 1982

ASSOCIATION OF TEACHERS OF MATHS *Points of Departure 1 & 2* ATM 1986

BAKER John & Ann *From puzzles to projects* Nelson 1986

BORBA Michele & Craig *Self Esteem: A Classroom Affair* Winston Press Inc., Minneapolis, USA 1978

BOTT B *Mathematical Activities* Cambridge University Press 1982

BOTT B *More Mathematical Activities* Cambridge University Press 19??

BURTON L *Thinking Things Through* Blackwell 1986

BUXTON L *Mathematics for Everyman* Dent 1984

CAMBOURNE B 'Language, learning and literacy' in BUTLER A and TURBILL J *Towards a reading/writing classroom* Primary English Teaching Association, NSW, 1984

CANFIELD Jack, WELLS Harold *101 Ways To Enhance Self-Concept In The Classroom* Englewood Hall, N.J. Prentice Hall 1976

CHIAK Mary, HERON Barbara *Games Children Should Play* Good Year Books, Scott, Foresman & Company, London 1980

COCKCROFT *Mathematics Counts* HMSO (London) 1985

CURRICULUM SERVICES UNIT *Drama Is Primary* Education Department of Victoria, Publications and Information Branch 1982

DALTON Joan *Adventures In Thinking* Thomas Nelson Australia 1985

DOIG B A (ed.) *Mathsbank* Mathematical Association of Victoria

DOIG B A (ed.) *Mathsbank II* Mathematical Association of Victoria 1985

EDUCATION DEPARTMENT OF SOUTH AUSTRALIA *Outdoor Education Activities and Games* Publications Branch 1978

EVANGELISTA A, HUNTING R, MORGAN M, WILSON D *Breaking Out—Theme Based Maths Activities* Maths Association of Victoria

FLEET Alma, MARTIN Lilian *Thinking It Through—Ideas for classroom organisation* Thomas Nelson Australia 1984

FLOYD A (ed.) *Developing Mathematical Thinking* Open University 1981

FLOYD A (ed.) *Games—games for the classroom and the playground* Collins Dove, Blackburn, Victoria 1987

The GETTING STARTED GROUP *Six Of The Best* Robert Andersen & Associates, Victoria 1986

HATCH G *Bounce to It—A collection of investigations for infants* Manchester Polytechnic, Didsbury, Manchester

HATCH G *Jump to It—A collection of investigations for 9–14 year olds* Manchester Polytechnic, Didsbury, Manchester

HMI *Mathematics from 5 to 16* HMSO (London) 1985

HUGHES M *Children and Number*

HUYTON et al *Mathematics Starting Points* Spartacus Educational 1988

KANICI C *Young children reinvent arithmetic* Teachers College Press, Columbia University 1985

LEES K *Sleuth—Stimulating Maths Investigations* Dellasta 1988

LOVITT Charles & CLARKE Doug *Maths Curriculum and Teaching Program* Vol 1, Curriculum Development Centre, Canberra, 1988

MACINTOSH A *Process Approach to Mathematics—Whence and Withers?* Australian Mathematics Teacher, April 1988

MATHEMATICAL ASSOCIATION OF WESTERN AUSTRALIA *100 Mathematics Problems* Mathematical Association of Western Australia 1980

MINISTRY OF EDUCATION, VICTORIA *Nursery Rime*

MOORE Peter *More Drama* Thomas Nelson Australia 1988

MOSCOVICH Ivan *Mind Benders—Games of Chance* Penguin 1986

MOSCOVICH Ivan *Mind Benders—Games of Shape* Penguin 1986

MOTTERSHEAD Lorraine *Investigations in Mathematics* McGraw-Hill 1985

MOTTERSHEAD Lorraine *Sources of Mathematical Discovery* Basil Blackwell 1977

NEVILLE L and DOWLING C *Let's Talk Turtle* and *How Turtles Talk* Cambridge University Press 1988

NOSS R et al *Microworlds—Adventures with* Logo Hutchinson 1987

PAPERT P *Mindstorms: Children, Computers and Powerful Ideas* Harvester Press 1980

PHILLIPS Dave *Mind-Boggling Mazes*

ROBINSON I *Mathematics and Language* Paper for Mathematics Language Conference, La Trobe University, July 1988

SHUARD H *Primary Mathematics Today and Tomorrow* Longman 1986

STEEN David *Aerobic Fun For Kids* Dove Communications, Blackburn, Victoria 1984

STOESSIGERS R *Using Language Conditions in Mathematics* Penguin (Australia) 1988

SWISS COMMITTEE FOR UNICEF *Games Of The World* Plenary Publications International Inc. 1982